A KILLER CHRISTMAS PARTY

A JILL ANDREWS COZY MYSTERY

NICOLE ELLIS

1

$\mathcal{I}$ ran my fingers over the glossy plastic cover of the binder I'd used to corral all of the details for the Pearson Company's Christmas party. My mother-in-law, Beth, had told me that they had a big to-do every year and she'd asked me to plan this year's event at the Boathouse Event Center. I'd met with their human resources manager and Harry Pearson himself a few times to discuss their ideas.

After many hours of hard work, I had put together a party I thought they'd love. I set the binder down on my desk and clicked on my computer's calendar to make sure I'd recorded all of the pertinent dates.

From outside of my closed office door came the high-pitched whine of little girls and then crashing as they ran amok in the hallway. A ribbon of irrational fear ran through me. They were here and I had no chance for escape. I'd hoped to be done with work for the day before my brother-in-law Will arrived with his wife and three girls, but the binder had taken me longer than I'd thought it would.

I frantically surveyed my desk. The nameplate reading

Jill Andrews, Events Coordinator would be fine, but having a cup of coffee so close to my computer was asking for trouble. I moved the coffee onto a high bookshelf out of reach of small children, then closed the lid of my laptop before shoving it into a desk drawer for safety. The binder was too thick to fit in my file drawers, so I set it on top of the file cabinet. When only unbreakables remained in view, I opened my door and peeked into the hall.

Like velociraptors, they sensed the open door. Two of my nieces ran toward me, their feet slapping against the hardwood floors with each step.

"Auntie Jill!" yelled Maya with her long dark hair flying behind her. She and her younger sister Claire came to a screeching halt in front of me.

"Hi, girls." I looked down the hall, but didn't see Will or Tania. "Where are your parents?"

"Daddy's in Grandma Beth's office and Mommy went to the spa. She said she was tired after the long trip." Claire bounced on the balls of her feet in front of me, her short bobbed haircut swirling around her thin face.

"Ah." I nodded. "And where is Bella?" When I'd seen her a year ago, my ten-year-old niece had been bouncing off the walls along with her younger sisters.

Claire sighed loudly. "She's reading."

"Again," said Maya. She nudged past me. "Is this your office? Can we see it?" She walked in before I even had a chance to answer.

"Uh, sure." I did another quick visual search of the room. "Go ahead. It's not that exciting."

They ran into the room, bumbling around behind the desk. Maya sat on my ergonomic swivel desk chair and spun it around until I was dizzy from watching her.

Claire immediately spotted the rubber bouncy ball I

kept in a basket in the corner for Mikey and Anthony to use when they came to visit. They loved throwing the ball down the empty hallway outside my office. She grabbed the ball and chucked it at her sister, who was now standing behind my desk.

Maya ducked and the ball ricocheted off of the file cabinet and onto the top of the bookshelf—directly at my coffee cup. The cup wobbled, then fell, spilling its contents over the edge of the top shelf and crashing to the ground where it broke into pieces.

I gasped and ran over to the binder I'd set carefully on top of the file cabinet. Dark brown coffee had sprayed over the shiny plastic surface and dripped onto the pages inside, staining them a lighter brown. I touched the soggy paper. All of that work for nothing. I couldn't show my client this.

Claire's eyes widened, but she said nothing. Maya giggled and threw the ball at her sister, who caught it mid-air. They both ran out into the hallway, their feet thundering against the floorboards with every move.

I had a little boy and I knew how quickly kids could make messes, but this was ridiculous. I stood there, staring at my ruined binder before I turned my attention to the glass shards of what used to be my favorite coffee cup. I picked up a large piece that contained only half of Thumper on it. Adam had bought it for me when we took a pre-kids trip to Disney World, and I'd loved it ever since.

I threw some paper towels down on the mess to sop up the liquid and walked to the Boathouse's linen closet to get something to mop up the rest of it. On the way there, I could hear the girls' voices bouncing down the hallway, followed closely by the rubber ball, which flew through the air and banged into my head. I pressed my lips together and tried to think rationally. It worked somewhat, and I retrieved the ball from the floor, tucking it under my arm.

"Hey, we were playing with that." Maya's mouth formed into an unbecoming pout.

I smiled sweetly at her. "Not anymore." I looked around. I still hadn't seen their dad, but he was probably with Beth in her office, which was near the kitchen.

When I walked past her office, I ducked my head in.

"Jill, hi." Will rose from his seat and came over to the door to hug me. It always amazed me how much he and Adam looked alike, with their sandy-brown hair and lanky statures. He peered at me. "You look frazzled."

I stepped back. He was acting differently than usual—nicer, maybe. Not that he'd ever been rude to me in the past, but his usual demeanor was closer to sleazy used-car salesman than a caring relative.

I wanted to scream at him that his kids had done that to me, but I refrained. "The girls were in my office and broke a mug filled with coffee, so I'm in search of cleaning supplies."

A frown crossed his face. "I'm so sorry, Jill. I'll talk to them about it. Maybe they can help you clean it up."

I was glad that he turned then toward the door so that he couldn't see the expression of horror that I knew was covering my face. He walked out of the room, leaving me alone with Beth.

"Isn't it great that Will and the kids are here?" Beth beamed at me.

"Yeah, it's really great." I tried to put some enthusiasm into my voice but I feared it fell flat. "It amazes me though how they can become little tornadoes."

She sighed. "I know. The girls have a lot of energy."

"Where's Bella anyway? She wasn't with her sisters."

"I think she's reading a book in the main room." Beth

shook her head. "She's changed a lot since I last saw her. I can't believe she'll be a teenager soon."

I grinned. "Not for another few years."

"It goes fast." Beth sighed again. "I wish they lived closer to us. I hate not seeing them more than twice a year."

I knew the feeling. It seemed like just yesterday Mikey had been a baby, and now he was four and a half. Even Ella had recently turned a year old. Where had the time gone?

I jutted my thumb at the door. "I'd better get back and clean up the mess before the coffee permanently stains everything."

She nodded. "Don't forget we're scheduled for dinner with everyone tonight. I'm making roast chicken—Will's favorite."

"I haven't forgotten." I wished I could "accidentally" forget, but I knew Adam would insist that we attend dinner with the whole family.

I retrieved the rags to wipe up the spilled coffee and glass and returned to my office. I was now behind in my work because, in addition to cleaning up the mess the girls had made, I'd have to redo the client binder. That was several hours of my life that I'd planned to use for Christmas shopping, but now I'd have to put that off until later.

I loved Christmas, but I was getting to the point in the year where it couldn't come and go fast enough. We always spent Christmas Eve with Adam's family as it was their big family get-together, but Christmas Day was spent with my family. My sister, Becky, who lived in Portland, Oregon, called me the night before to inform me that she'd be coming up to visit us on Christmas Day and to ask if it was ok if she stayed a while afterward. She and her husband had recently split up and she wanted to spend the holidays with us.

Of course, I'd felt obligated to invite her to stay with us, but now I was struggling to figure out where I'd put everyone. My parents were planning on staying with us from Christmas Day through New Year's too, and although we had a nice-sized house, it would get crowded with three extra people in it for a week.

As I threw the shards of glass into a paper sack and then into the plastic trash bag, I reflected on how quickly things could change. Last Christmas, Ella had only been a few months old and she'd been bewildered by our holiday celebrations. Less than a year later, she was toddling around, Desi had given birth to a little girl too, my parents had almost gotten a divorce, Becky had separated from her husband, and Adam and I had both started new jobs. Nothing stayed the same and I wasn't sure whether I liked that or not.

I tied the bag and set it next to the door to take out to the outside garbage dumpster, then opened the metal rings on the white binder. Page by page, I laid the materials out on my desk and when that was filled, I set some on the bookshelf. About half of them were damaged, but the other half would be fine. I breathed a sigh of relief. If I hurried, I might be able to fix everything before we needed to leave for dinner at Beth's house that evening.

Two hours later, the project was salvaged, and I drove home to change out of my work clothes and get ready for dinner. As I threw on a pair of jeans and a sweater, Goldie, our golden retriever, stared at me forlornly from the bed where he lay stretched out with his head on his front paws.

"I'll try to take you for a quick walk when I get home, ok, boy?" I smoothed the long green knit sweater down over my hips and ruffled the fur on his head. He lifted his head briefly, then set it back down. I hadn't been home as much lately as I used to be, and even the dog was getting in on the guilt trips. Ordinarily, Beth would let me bring him over to her house when we went there for family dinners, but with all of the extra people staying there, I didn't think it was a good idea. Besides, I wasn't sure how my sister-in-law Tania felt about dogs. I had a hunch she wasn't fond of them.

"Honey," Adam called up the stairs. "Are you ready yet? We were supposed to be there five minutes ago."

"In a minute," I shouted back. I swiped some concealer under my eyes to hide the bags that were forming there and brushed my hair until it gleamed like a copper penny. My sister-in-law always looked like she'd stepped out of the pages of a magazine, and although I'd never be able to compete with her, or want to for that matter, I didn't want to look like a complete mess either.

I grabbed my coat from where I'd tossed it on the ground when I'd rushed upstairs and took a deep breath while looking in the mirror. I'd make it through this dinner somehow.

2

My feet were full of lead as I walked out to the car with Ella. Mikey was skipping along next to us, excited to see the cousins he barely knew. His cousin Anthony, Desi's son, would be there too, but Mikey got to see him almost every day at preschool, so he wasn't a novelty like Will's kids were. Rain had started to fall, speckling the cement sidewalks with an array of dark spots.

"Maybe we could claim that Ella isn't feeling well?" My earlier resolve was failing already and I crossed my fingers that Adam would consider my excuse to miss dinner at his parents' house. I didn't think he'd go for it though as he'd been talking lately about wanting to spend more time with Will. They hadn't been close since they were children, but Adam hoped to fix that. Will and Tania had never been overly friendly to me, although when I'd seen him earlier that day, he'd surprised me.

Adam shot me an icy death glare as he opened the door so I could place Ella in her rear-facing car seat. "We're going."

I sighed. "Fine."

He softened a little. "Look, I know the girls are a bit much, and Tania can be prickly, but they're my family and I haven't seen Will in over a year. Can you please put up with them for a few hours?"

I instantly felt guilty. After all, the girls were just little kids. "I will. I'm sorry. I know they didn't mean to break my mug or ruin my binder." I'd given Adam a quick rundown of my day when he'd checked on me while I was getting ready for dinner.

He laughed. "They probably did, but they're still family and we're stuck with them, like it or not."

We drove to Beth and Lincoln's house and pulled up behind Desi's car and what appeared to be a late model luxury rental car. The lights were on in the living room and I could see people moving around. We were definitely last to arrive.

Adam rang the doorbell with Mikey beside him and I trudged up the sidewalk behind them while carrying Ella.

"Remember, be nice," he whispered.

"Yeah, Mom, be nice," Mikey echoed helpfully.

At that very moment, the door opened and Will appeared. Had he heard Mikey? My face grew warm and to hide it, I leaned down to set Ella on the ground.

"It's good to see you, baby brother," Will said, hugging Adam affectionately.

Adam hugged him back. "It's been too long."

Will crouched down to be eye to eye with Ella. "And this must be Ella? You were just a little baby last time I saw you."

She eyed him with suspicion and clung to my leg for dear life.

He laughed. "Mikey, the girls are looking forward to seeing you." He gestured behind him. "They're downstairs in the family room."

Mikey bounded off and I heard his cousin Anthony shout an excited greeting to him.

"It's so nice that you were able to be here for Christmas this year," I said to Will.

He hugged me for the second time that day. I was starting to wonder what alien had taken over my brother-in-law's body. "I wanted the girls to be around family." His face turned down. "We love Arizona, but I want them to grow up around relatives."

Adam caught that. "Are you thinking of moving back to Washington?"

Will started to walk down the hallway toward the living room. "I'm thinking about it, but we haven't made any decisions yet."

I groaned inwardly. Having the girls around full-time would change the dynamics of our family and I kind of liked it the way it was. *They need their family too, Jill*, a little voice said. It was true. I loved having relatives close by us and they deserved the same.

"That would be great," I said. "Your parents would love it."

He didn't answer because we'd entered the living room where my in-laws and Tania were seated.

Beth jumped up. "Do you want something to drink? We've got beer, wine, soda, or water, of course."

Adam grinned. "I'm fine, Mom. Since when am I a proper guest in your house?"

"Well, Jill might want something," she said defensively.

"A glass of water would be great." I smiled. Beth seemed anxious to do something, perhaps to avoid talking to Tania.

Beth left and I sat down in a chair that was diagonal from Tania.

"How was your flight out here?" I asked.

"Horrible." She slugged back her wine, draining the glass. "The kids were awful, the flight was bumpy, and now I'm here in Seattle and it's raining." She looked out the window at the drizzle. I think she was trying to scowl, but her skin was so frozen with Botox that I couldn't tell for sure. "I hate rain. So depressing."

I wasn't sure how to respond. I hadn't interacted with Tania much in the past, but when I had, she hadn't been quite so negative. I'd never seen her happy though, except maybe at her wedding, and even then she'd spent the day ordering Will around. Having the wedding at the Boathouse hadn't been her first choice, but Will had insisted they have it there. To retaliate, she'd made all the staff miserable with her demands.

Beth re-entered the room, saving me from talking to Tania. "Dinner's almost ready," she announced as she handed me a glass that was filled to the brim with ice and water.

I took it from her, my fingers instantly becoming chilled from the cool glass. "Thanks. What are we having for dinner? I know you told me earlier, but my mind is like a sieve lately."

She laughed. "It's Christmas mom-brain. We're having roast chicken, mashed potatoes, green beans, a side salad, and homemade rolls. It's Will's favorite." She beamed at her oldest son. "I made the potatoes with only half of the usual amount of butter, because I know how healthy Tania likes to eat." She wrinkled her nose. "I hope they taste ok."

I glanced at Tania, who was examining her fingernails. She didn't appear to have noticed her mother-in-law's comments.

Beth sat down on the edge of the couch next to Lincoln.

"Will said he had big news. Will—do you want to tell us now before the kids come upstairs?"

"I wouldn't say it was big news. It's not really anything at the moment." He picked up his drink from an end table and took a sip.

Tania looked up at her husband. "What is it?"

He met her gaze. "I've been thinking about moving up here and buying a bed-and-breakfast on Willowby Island. A friend of mine is selling theirs and it would be a great opportunity."

My head shot up. Did Tania not know about this plan? If not, fireworks were about to go off.

Her reaction didn't disappoint.

She stared at him wide-eyed. "You can't be serious. We have a life in Arizona. I have friends, the kids have friends. We're close to my family in Nevada and you have a thriving dermatology practice. We can't just pick up and leave. That's insane."

He held up his hands. "Now, just wait. I didn't say I'd decided for sure. I still need to visit the B and B while we're up here for Christmas."

I thought her eyes were going to fall out of her head.

"You made plans to see the place without even asking me how I felt about moving."

Will focused his attention on the burgundy floral rug. "You know how much I hate dermatology. I've been telling you that for years, but I've stuck it out because I know how much you love the money."

Beth's eyes were going back and forth between Will and Tania, almost as though they were players in a tennis match. Lincoln looked like he'd rather be anywhere other than in his own living room at the moment and I felt the same way.

Tania stood and marched over to Will. "When I married

you, you were a dermatologist with a promising career ahead of you. You can't just change everything now. And I'm definitely not going to become some hostess at a B and B." She walked over to the end of the couch and snagged her purse, which she slung roughly over her shoulder. "You forced us to come up here for Christmas and now you spring this on me? I'm out of here." She flounced out of the room, the front door slamming as she exited the house.

We all stared at each other. For the second time that night, I was at a loss for the right words.

"Ahem." Adam cleared his throat and turned to Will. "Is that true? You want to quit your job and run a B and B?"

Will nodded. "I thought being a doctor would allow me to connect with patients, but I only see them for a brief visit and then in surgery. I want to be around people that are awake—actually get to know them. And Willowby Island has always had a special place in my heart. I remember when we used to go camping near the beach there when we were kids."

Adam nodded. "I remember. I loved it too." He peered at his brother. "It sounds like you've made up your mind."

Will sighed. "I would love to jump at the chance to own the B and B, but Tania pretty much reacted the way I thought she would. I know I should have told her earlier, but I hoped she'd at least consider it if I told her about it with a bunch of people around." His eyes were downcast. "Imagine how great it would be for the kids to grow up on Willowby Island. It would be so different from Arizona. They'd get to play outdoors in the trees and grass, and not be stuck inside with air-conditioning all year."

Lincoln and Beth exchanged glances.

"We thought you loved living in Arizona," Beth said. "You've never mentioned anything different."

"I didn't tell anyone because you were dealing with your own health problems, but a couple of months ago, I had a health scare of my own."

I heard Beth's sharp intake of breath. "Are you ok?"

He smiled at her. "Yes, Mom, I'm fine. It was a false alarm, but it really made me think. I don't want to continue living the way we have been, away from family and me not ever having time to spend with my kids."

Lincoln nodded. "Ok. So what can we do to help? It doesn't sound like Tania's on board with all of this."

"No, but I think she'll come around." Will was trying to sound confident, but he looked uncertain.

A timer in the kitchen binged and Beth jumped up. "Dinner's ready."

Adam stood and called down the stairs, "Kids, time to wash up for dinner."

They thundered up the stairs and jostled past each other to get to the bathroom sink first. We ate dinner together as a family, but Will's kids asked several times about their mother's absence, putting a strain on the rest of the evening. When Adam called it a night, I didn't protest in the slightest.

3

The next morning, Mikey's preschool class was scheduled to bring handmade Christmas cards to a retirement home where they would sing a few carols for the residents. Adam had a client meeting, so I stopped by Beth's house to drop Ella off for a few hours.

I rang the doorbell of my in-laws' house, clutching Ella in my arms. Since I'd only be gone for a minute, I'd let Mikey stay in the car behind me in the driveway. When Beth opened the door, her face was haggard and she was gently rocking Desi's baby daughter, Lina.

"Hey," she said in a tired voice. "How's Miss Ella this morning?"

"She's doing well," I said, looking down at Ella, who stood clutching my leg. "But you don't look so good. Are you ok?"

"Oh sure. I'm fine. It's just been a bit much with having Will's girls here." She shook her head. "They're so full of energy."

I cocked my head to the side. "Aren't Will and Tania here to take care of them?"

NICOLE ELLIS

"Will had a late night out last night, and Tania never came home." She shook her head again. "I don't know what's going on between those two." She glanced back into the house and whispered to me, "He might be better off without her though."

I bit my lip. Hearing my mother-in-law speak badly of my sister-in-law was always a shock because Beth was one of the nicest people in the world. Tania must have really rubbed her the wrong way.

As if she'd read my mind, Beth added hastily, "I shouldn't have said that. Please forget I said anything."

I smiled. "Of course. I knew what you meant." I knew she'd meant what she'd said, but I didn't want to make her feel bad about it.

I glanced back at Mikey. "I'd better get going to the retirement home. Mikey worked for an hour on his Christmas card and he's excited to sing for the retirees."

"Have fun." Beth waved to Mikey in the car. "You're picking up Ella after work, right?"

"Yeah, unless you need me to come and get her earlier." I scrutinized her face. "Are you sure you're all right with all of the girls?" Beth often watched Lina and Ella and sometimes Anthony and Mikey as well without breaking a sweat, but Will's girls were a different matter.

"Don't worry about it. Will should be waking up soon and then he can take care of his girls. I think he'd planned to take them to the zoo today anyway."

"Ok then." I peered past her into the house, where I heard two of the girls shouting at each other. Beth had said she'd be fine though and I needed to get going with Mikey now so we could arrive at the retirement home in time to sing. Nancy Davenport, the leader of the Busy Bees

Preschool PTA, would never let me forget it if I showed up late.

I got back into the car with Mikey and we drove to the part of town along the bluff overlooking Puget Sound. Most of the houses in this stretch of the road had been built around the early 1900s for wealthy settlers. I'd been here recently when I'd visited Angela Deveaux's house, but I'd never been to the retirement home before. As we motored past her house, I shuddered, thinking about the body I'd found there just before Halloween. The house and lawn were well-kept, but nothing had been decorated for Christmas. Poor Angela. Being all alone in that big house couldn't be fun, especially knowing that her husband killed someone on their property and had tried to murder her as well.

Ericksville Heights Retirement Home was housed in a large building from the early 1900s. From the size of it, I'd guess it had originally been a hotel for the well-to-do. In preparation for Christmas, someone had strung up lights along the roofline and decorated a tall pine tree in the front yard. Christmas wasn't too far away, and I mentally moved decorating up a few spots on my to-do list. Maybe Adam and I could put the lights up over the next weekend.

The parking for the retirement home was across a residential street from the house. The lot was packed, and Mikey and I had to park at the far edge of it. I checked the time on the car's clock. We were already a minute late and I still had to get him out of the car and over to the home.

"Ok, Mikey, grab your card and let's go." He started to unfasten his seatbelt and I opened the minivan's side door to help him out.

"My coat?" he asked, pointing at his puffy blue winter jacket.

I shook my head. That would add several minutes on to

our timeline. I hadn't bothered to put mine on either, and it wasn't too far to the building.

Together, we ran across the street, past a sign reading *Ericksville Heights Retirement Home* and up the front steps of the large building.

I opened the door and a blast of heat welcomed us.

"Welcome," a young woman behind the desk sang out in a too-cheery voice. She pointed toward the back of the lobby. "You're here with the preschool, right?"

I nodded and she went back to her computer.

In front of us, twenty preschoolers and their parents bumbled around the front desk and a very overwhelmed looking woman in her early twenties. I caught sight of Desi and Anthony, and we joined them where they stood on the outskirts of the crowd.

"Thank goodness. I thought they'd have started by now," I whispered to Desi.

"No. The recreation director for the retirement home didn't show up at work today and her assistant isn't very well prepared for this. Nancy's fit to be tied."

I snuck a peek over at Nancy. Her face was pink and her hands waved haphazardly in the air as she berated the poor assistant.

"I'm glad I'm not on the receiving end of that." We waited a few minutes and then the young woman led us into a room filled with senior citizens.

"Good morning, everyone," the assistant said in a low voice that no one heard. She cleared her throat and tried again. "Good morning."

This time a few eyes turned to her and she smiled. The room quieted.

"As you may know, we have a special treat for you today.

The children from Busy Beavers Preschool have come to share some Christmas cards with you and sing."

"Bees," Nancy called out. "We're from Busy Bees Preschool." She shook her head in disgust.

"Yes, of course." The woman's face fell for a moment, but she quickly recovered. "Let's welcome the kids from Busy Bees Preschool."

We all nudged our children forward and they gathered in a ramshackle line, then belted out an off-key version of "We Wish You a Merry Christmas." The crowd cheered politely and they sang a few more Christmas carols, then disbanded. Led by the parents, the kids then spread out and joined some of the senior citizens at their tables.

"Oh look, there's Delilah Brown," Desi said.

"Who?" I scanned the room for anyone vaguely familiar.

As she walked toward the back of the room, she pointed out a woman sitting among friends at a round table. "She's one of Mom's friends at the Ericksville Historical Society. I've known her my whole life." She paused. "You remember you're helping out at the historical homes tour this weekend, right?"

I felt my stomach lurch. I'd forgotten promising Beth that I'd volunteer at it. She wasn't able to make it because of commitments at the Boathouse and had begged me to help out. Since she did so much for Adam and I, there was no way I could say no to her request. There went any chance of decorating this weekend.

I pasted a smile on my face. "Of course."

Desi lifted an eyebrow at me, but said nothing.

I followed her dutifully over to the woman's table.

"Hi, Delilah." Desi leaned down to give her a small hug. "I was hoping I'd see you today."

The woman beamed. "I wouldn't miss it for anything.

This is the highlight of the Christmas season." The women beside her nodded.

"We love seeing all the kids," one woman with a cloud of fluffy white hair said. "And who are these little angels?"

I almost looked around the room for said angels before realizing she meant our boys.

Desi pointed at Anthony, who was staring at the women with wide eyes. "This is my son, Anthony, and my nephew, Mikey." She turned to Delilah. "And this is my sister-in-law, Jill. She's married to Adam."

"Ah," Delilah said, "so nice to meet you, Jill. I'll have to tell Beth I finally had a chance to make your acquaintance."

I smiled at her. "It's nice to meet you too."

The other women stood to leave. "We're going to go to the chair yoga class now. Do you want to join us, Delilah?"

Delilah shook her head. "No, not today." After they left, she asked us, "Would you like to join me for a coffee break in the dining room?"

I glanced at Mikey, who was bouncing restlessly behind the table.

"There are cookies for coffee break," Delilah said. "And they're delicious."

The boys heard the word cookies.

"Can we, Mommy?" Anthony asked, his eyes dancing with thoughts of cookies.

Desi laughed. "Sure, we'd love to join you."

"Great." Delilah stood with the aid of her walker and guided us slowly toward a large dining area. "The cookies are over there and they'll serve us coffee at the table." She chortled softly. "They don't think it's a good idea for us old folks to be carrying cups of hot coffee while using our walkers. Can't say I blame them though."

Once we'd chosen our treats and had been served coffee

and milk, the boys munched away happily at their plates of cookies. Desi and I had allowed them to splurge on several cookies each in hopes that it would occupy them while we chatted with Delilah.

"I love your walker." Desi pointed to Delilah's walker, which was decked out with hot pink tennis balls on the bottom and shiny silver streamers hanging from the handles.

She laughed and ran her fingers through the streamers. "I can't resist the urge to make things pretty."

"So how long have you lived in Ericksville?" I asked, sipping my hot coffee.

"All my life," she said proudly. "I've been here since it was a sleepy little town, before we even had a proper ferry."

"Wow. You must have some tales to tell," I said. "I'm curious, was this building originally a hotel?"

She laughed, a wonderful tinkling sound. "Yes. It was built as a hotel, then became a sanatorium. After tuberculosis became less prevalent, it was turned into apartments, and most recently, of course, the Ericksville Heights Retirement Home." She looked around the room with pride. "It's beautiful, isn't it?"

Desi nodded her head. "It is. I've always admired the building."

"I just love living in a building with so much history," Delilah said as she crunched down on a Santa Claus–shaped Christmas cookie. When she finished, she told us a bit more about the home's heritage. "You know, there's a rumor that during Prohibition, the owners of the sanatorium were rumrunners. They'd fill their boat with alcohol in Canada and come down here to distribute it."

"I've never heard about rumrunners in Ericksville

before," Desi said. "I'll have to see if my mom knows anything about that."

Delilah regaled us with more tales about the area's history. I was fascinated by how much she knew of the area and could have listened to her for hours. Having grown up in Idaho, I didn't know much about Ericksville's past.

Unfortunately, ten minutes later, Mikey and Anthony were on the last crumbs of cookie, and I knew they wouldn't sit there so patiently for much longer.

"We'd better get going," I said.

"So soon?" Delilah asked.

Desi smiled at her gently. "We need to get the kids to preschool and I have to get back to the café."

"Oh, that's right. I forgot you own a café." Delilah looked at me. "And what about you?"

"I've been working with Beth at the Boathouse since last spring as an event coordinator."

"Oh, how fun," she said. "Beth always has the best stories about some of the Boathouse clients. Do you like it?" She peered at me.

"I do. I've found I enjoy coordinating events for people. I used to be in marketing but in a behind the scenes capacity. Getting to actually know some of the clients has been great." That was mainly true, although there were a few exceptions —Angela and a couple of Bridezillas came to mind. Thinking about work reminded me that I still needed to get the final count for the Pearson Company's Christmas party, which was my first priority after I got back to the office that day.

The boys were starting to jostle each other and get louder. Desi and I stood.

"It was nice to meet you, Delilah," I said, grabbing Mikey's hand firmly. He squirmed, trying to escape my grip.

Desi hugged her. "I'll try to stop in and see you again soon. This was nice."

"That would be lovely," Delilah said to Desi, then turned to me. "It was nice meeting you, Jill. I'd love to see both of you again." Her voice held notes of sadness. "Say, before you go, would it be ok with you if I give the boys each a piece of candy?" She held up a roll of cherry LifeSavers.

I smiled. "Sure. I think they'd like that."

Delilah removed two pieces of candy and gave one to each of them. The boys took them eagerly and immediately stuck the treats in their mouths.

We waved goodbye and led the kids outside. They ran over to a line of hedges that bordered one side of the yard, darting in and out of them while giggling.

"We should probably stop them," I said half-heartedly.

"Yeah, probably. But I don't think they're hurting anything and they're having fun. They had to be quiet for so long in the retirement home that they need a little playtime outside."

"I'm glad we were able to have coffee with Delilah though," I said. "I really liked her."

"Me too. Like I said, I've known her my whole life." She frowned. "I didn't realize how lonely she was though."

"If you'd like, I wouldn't mind visiting her again. Maybe we could even pick her up and bring her to the café for coffee."

Desi smiled. "I like that idea. Remind me about it after Christmas, ok? Things should be calmer by then."

As we stood on the front walkway, she pointed at the brightly lit Christmas tree. "They outdid themselves with the tree."

She was right. It was decorated in a mix of multi-colored lights, with delicate metal stars twisted in between them.

"I wonder why the building isn't lit up too?" I stared up at the eaves. Small colorful bulbs hung off of the gutters, but they weren't on. "It must look pretty at night." With its multiple stories and fanciful architecture lit up against the darkness of Puget Sound behind it, the retirement home would be magnificently beautiful.

Before she could answer, we both noticed that it was quiet—too quiet.

"Where are the boys?" My eyes roved over the hedges and the rest of the grounds in front of the building, but I didn't spot them.

"I don't know. I told Anthony not to run off." Desi stalked over to the hedges and looked over the top of them to the other side. "They're not here."

I put my hand on my hip and sighed. "Mikey's getting bad about it too. He thinks he knows everything and is getting way too independent. He even left a store one day without me and I found him waiting outside after I spent a few frantic minutes searching for him."

I put my hand over my eyes to block the sun's glare and surveyed the yard again. I didn't see them in the street or the parking lot, but that left only one place—the back of the building.

The sound of little boys' high-pitched laughter rang out from the backyard.

"There's a fence along the bluff, right?" I asked. Fear replaced annoyance, and my words cracked. I wouldn't put it past Mikey to go right up to the edge of the cliff, much like he had when we were at a lake resort back in August.

"I don't know," Desi said grimly. "We'd better find out."

I ran over to the side of the building closest to the hedges, but a fence without a gate blocked the way.

I pointed to the far side of the yard. "We have to go around the other way."

We jetted around the other side to the back of the building. I sighed with relief when I spotted the boys playing around a statue in the middle of a garden that must have been beautiful when it bloomed in the spring and summer. In the winter, it was still pleasant, but in a frozen tundra kind of way.

I started to call out to the boys, but tripped over a shoe before I could say anything. What was a ladies red patent leather pump with a two-inch heel doing out here in the middle of the grass? My eyes caught on another flash of red about five feet away. What was going on? Something swayed above me, casting a gray shadow on the building. I looked up to see what it was and gasped, covering my mouth with my hand before I could scream.

4

---

*A*bove us, in between some dormer windows, a woman hung by her neck from a thick mess of tangled Christmas lights. Her lifeless eyes stared downward at us.

I froze in disbelief. What a horrible way to die.

"Desi," I hissed.

"I know," she said without turning to look at me. "I'll get them down from there." The boys were now playing on the statue.

"Leave them."

Now she turned. "What? They could damage it."

I pointed upward and her eyes followed, widening when she saw what was hanging from the roof.

"Oh, my goodness. That's horrible." She was quiet for a moment. "Do you think she was hanging the lights?"

"I don't know. But we've got to tell someone." I shivered. That was why I never liked to put the Christmas lights on our house. I was terrified of falling.

We both looked at the boys, who were completely oblivious to what was going on thirty feet away from them.

"I don't think she's going anywhere. Let's go inside with the boys and we can let the front desk know." I moved closer to the boys so they weren't likely to see the body and called out, "Boys! Time to go." They must have sensed the urgency in my voice, because they trotted over to us without protest.

We walked back into the building. The receptionist's cheery smile fell when she saw our troubled faces.

"Is something wrong?" she asked.

The boys had already started chatting with an elderly man about his cane, so we both moved closer to the reception desk.

"There's a woman's body hanging from the roof in the back of the building," I said in a hushed voice.

Her mouth gaped open. "Excuse me?"

"You need to call the police," Desi said, her words slow and patient enough for a small child to comprehend. "There's been an accident. It looks like she fell off of the building while hanging Christmas lights."

"Oh my. Are you sure? Is she ok? The maintenance crew installed the lights yesterday morning. I can't imagine why anyone would be up there today."

I shook my head. "No. She's dead, I'm afraid."

She picked up her phone and dialed, then spoke to the 911 operator. After she hung up, her face was white as a sheet. "They'll be here in a few minutes. I can't believe this. I mean, I'm used to calling 911 when a resident has a medical emergency, but this is horrible." Her eyes filled with concern. "Wait, did the woman have dark hair?"

I thought back to the woman's hair that the wind had twisted into the lights. "Yes." I peered at her. "Why? Do you know who it is?"

"I don't know. I hope not," she said in a low voice. "But our recreation director is a bit of a perfectionist and I heard her complaining yesterday about how sloppy the maintenance crew had been when they hung the lights on the building. She has long, dark brown hair."

I looked over at Desi. Realization dawned in her eyes at the same time as mine.

"That would explain why she wasn't here today for the Christmas carols," she said.

The receptionist's eyes filled with tears. "Oh, poor Mila."

From the street, the sound of sirens filtered in through the walls. Half of the residents in the lobby turned toward the sound, probably worried that something had happened to one of their own.

A few minutes later, a policeman entered the lobby and approached the front desk. "Could I please speak to whoever found the body?"

"That would be us." Desi gestured to me as she came forward.

"We need to talk with you outside." He eyed the residents, who were on full alert.

"We have our kids with us," I said. "They got away from us earlier and that's why we were in the backyard, but we managed to keep them away from where she ... is. I don't want them to see her."

He looked at the kids. "I'll call someone in to look after them." He said something into his radio and a young policeman entered the room.

"I'll watch them while you go outside. Is that all right with you?" he asked us politely. With his curly blond hair and cherubic face, I wondered how long he'd been with the police force—and how much experience he had with kids. I gauged his expression and he didn't appear to be terrified of children, so I figured he'd be ok with them for a few minutes.

We nodded. "Thank you," I said.

The three of us went outside and around to the back of the building, where emergency personnel had gathered.

A photographer was already taking pictures of the scene.

"I'm going to need your information," the policeman said gruffly.

We provided him with our names and contact information and then I looked more closely at what was going on in front of us.

"Is all this necessary?" I pointed at the photographer.

"It is. Any time we have a suspicious death, we treat the scene with care," he said. "And this death is definitely suspicious."

Desi tipped her head to the side. "Why do you say that? It looked like she'd fallen while hanging the lights."

He sighed. "Did either of you see a ladder earlier?"

Ice ran through my veins. We'd checked the front of the building for the boys before heading around to the back and there hadn't been a ladder in front or on either of the sides.

"No. I didn't see one out front."

I saw Desi running her eyes along the base of the rear of the retirement home.

"Or back here," Desi said grimly. "But she must have climbed up a ladder to get up there. There's no other way to the roof."

Desi was right. None of the windows afforded much of a perch for climbing onto the roof. The ladder the woman had climbed was missing, and ladders didn't just walk off on their own. This hadn't been an accident.

"Somebody took the ladder," Desi said out loud.

The policeman didn't respond to her comment. "Did you notice anything suspicious when you were back here? You said that your children came around back first. Could they have played with the ladder?"

I would have laughed if the situation hadn't been so grim. Our four-year-olds wouldn't have been capable of carrying a heavy ladder long enough to reach the roof of a three-story building. "No. They couldn't have moved it very far away."

"And they weren't back here for very long," Desi added quickly. "Only a few minutes."

He jotted something down in his notebook. "Thank you for your time. Please stay nearby for a little longer in case we have any questions."

We nodded in unison.

He walked away from us, toward a few police officers standing in a group. They'd erected a yellow caution tape barrier, and behind it stood a dozen senior citizens who were watching the scene intently.

"That's Mila," one man said. "I knew something was wrong when she didn't show up today. She's always so dependable."

"But didn't maintenance hang the lights yesterday? Why would she be up there?" a woman asked.

Another said, "It must have happened last night. That's the Christmas sweater with the penguins on it that she wore yesterday."

Delilah came over to us. "I didn't know you girls were still here. It's awful, isn't it? She was so young and full of life."

"It is," Desi agreed.

After documenting the scene, the police carefully cut the woman's body down and lowered it to the ground. Mila's red and green Christmas sweater sagged into the frosty grass, the black penguins gazing forlornly up into the air. A tear slipped down Delilah's cheek and she wiped it away with a Kleenex that she removed from the sleeve of her sweater.

"They're saying she was murdered," she said in wonder. "Who would have wanted to kill Mila? She had no enemies."

"I don't know." I felt helpless watching her cry and wasn't sure how to comfort her.

Desi wrapped her arm around Delilah's hunched shoulders. "I'm sure the police will figure it out."

"I hope so. They haven't been much help with everything else going on around here." She blew her nose loudly.

My ears perked up, but before I could ask her what she meant, Mikey ran up to me and tugged on my arm.

"Can we go now?" he whined. "I want to go play at school."

The young policeman jogged out to us, his face contrite. "Sorry, ma'am. They escaped."

"Yeah, they're good at that," Desi said while gripping Anthony's hand. "Do you know if we're allowed to leave? The officer we spoke to had asked us to wait, but we need to get the boys off to preschool. I'm sure you don't want to watch them for much longer."

Terror filled his eyes at the mention of minding the boys again. "I'll go ask." He hurried over to the older police officer and spoke with him, then came back to us. "He said it's fine to go."

Desi patted Delilah on the shoulder. "I'm so sorry for your loss. Mila sounds like she was a good friend to everyone here."

"She was," Delilah said softly.

"We need to go now, but I'll come check on you later, ok?" Desi looked into Delilah's eyes.

Delilah nodded. "Thank you."

We said goodbye to her and walked toward the front of the building. I glanced back at Mila's body, which was still on the ground, but now covered with a special plastic tarp. We'd come to the retirement home for a preschool field trip and were now involved with yet another murder investigation. How was this happening?

After I dropped Mikey off at school, I returned to the Boathouse and worked through the afternoon finishing up details on the Pearson Company Christmas party. At five, I picked up Mikey and then stopped at Beth's house to get Ella.

When she opened the door, she looked better than she had that morning, but still tired. I made a mental note to increase our babysitter's schedule so I wouldn't have to depend on Beth so much.

"Hey, Jill," she said. "Come in, don't let the heat escape. Ella's in baby jail in the living room."

I followed her inside the house to where my daughter and Lina were sitting inside of a series of interlocked plastic fence pieces, playing with a plastic elephant that lit up when they pressed its buttons.

She pulled herself up on the fence when she saw me and babbled happily. Beth lifted her to freedom and set her down on the floor, where she promptly toddled over to me.

"Ella, Lina, and I had a good time once the older girls left with Will."

I looked around the living room. Everything looked ok, so Will's kids hadn't managed to break anything of Beth's. Lucky her.

I picked up Ella. "Did they end up going to the zoo? It seems cold to go there."

Beth nodded. "They went to the zoo and the Space Needle. Will is playing tourist, I think in hopes of convincing the girls of the benefits of living in Washington."

"Did Tania come back?" I wasn't sure if it was a good thing to ask, considering Beth's feelings about my sister-in-law, but curiosity got the best of me.

"She came back and got her stuff, then left promptly."

"She left?"

"Yep. She's decided to stay at a friend's house in Seattle for a few days."

"Is she coming back?"

Beth shrugged. "I don't know. I figured it wasn't my place to pry into things between her and Will."

"Yeah, that was probably best. I wonder what they'll tell the girls."

"I don't know. I'm not sure that the younger girls have noticed anything is wrong, but I think Bella has. She's barely poked her nose out of a book the whole time she's been here. She's changed a lot since I last saw her." She peered at me. "How did everything go at work today?"

I sighed. "Fine. The Pearson Company keeps coming up with more things to add to their Christmas party. Now they want to have reindeer munching on hay outside for the guests to see."

She raised an eyebrow. "Reindeer?"

"Yep. I told them I'd look into it, but I don't think I can pull it off for them."

"Well, good luck with all of that." She smothered a smile, then looked behind her into the kitchen. "I'd better get the kitchen cleaned up before everyone gets home. I'll see you at work tomorrow, ok?"

"Yes. Thanks again for watching Ella. I really appreciate it."

"No problem. I'm sure the residents at the retirement home appreciated the preschool's visit."

"I think they did." I didn't tell her about finding Mila's body. She had enough on her plate with Will and his family's drama. "See you tomorrow." I helped Ella wave goodbye to her grandma, and we let ourselves out of the house.

5

The next day, Adam had the morning free from client meetings, so he took Ella to the grocery store and Mikey to preschool. Overnight, I'd thought of a dozen more things I needed to do at work. The human resources manager from the Pearson Company had e-mailed me to increase their head count, so I needed to up their food order and check to make sure the seating plan would allow for the extra people. I also needed to call the company we'd used before for a horse and carriage rental to see if they had any reindeer in their stable.

When I arrived at the Boathouse, I ducked my head into the catering kitchen. They were hard at work preparing food for an event that afternoon and with the radio going, the noise was deafening. I beckoned to our catering manager, Lizzie, to meet me at the door.

She walked over to me briskly. "What's up, Jill?"

I smiled at her. "Remember how the Pearson Company wanted to increase the head count for their party a few weeks ago?"

"Yeah, why? We've already upped the order with our supplier. Do they want to cut that now?"

"No, they want to add even more people. Apparently more families have RSVP'd than they'd expected. Can we accommodate them?"

She thought about it for a moment. "We should be fine. I'll check our order and see what will need to change."

I beamed. Having such an organized catering manager made my life easier. "Thanks, Lizzie."

"No problem." She jutted her thumb toward the people scurrying around the kitchen behind her. "I'd better get back to supervising. Let me know if anything else changes with their party."

"I will, thanks."

She turned around and hurried back to the others. Thinking about the tasks that lay ahead in my workday, I walked down the hall to my office. If only the reindeer thing would be as easy as that had been.

I worked through the morning, then left to take my lunch break at the BeansTalk Café. I'd struck out with every place I'd considered for procuring reindeer and I was in need of a pick-me-up before calling the Pearson Company to let them know I wouldn't be able to provide reindeer for their party.

Desi was behind the counter, working alongside her assistant, Andrea, when I came in. She looked like she was going to jump out of her skin wanting to tell me something, but there were other customers ahead of me. When I got to the front of the line, she took my order of a turkey and cheddar on whole wheat, then said, "Don't go until I talk to you. I have to tell you something."

I regarded her with curiosity, but she just handed me my order and moved on to the next customer. Although the

BeansTalk was packed with customers, including a book club and some students on laptops, I managed to score a small table near the back. When the line had died down, Desi left Andrea alone at the counter and came over to where I was eating.

She slid into the chair opposite and leaned over the table to whisper to me. "The police think Will killed Mila. He came in earlier to tell me. He was so shaken up about it."

My head moved forward like a turtle's and my eyes widened so much that they hurt. "What? Why would they think that? Did he even know her?"

"Yeah. Will dated her in high school for a while. It didn't even occur to me because I haven't seen her in years and I was only in middle school when they were together. I was so wrapped up in myself that I didn't take much interest in the girls my brothers dated."

"Did they both date a lot? How many girls did Adam date?" It probably wasn't the most appropriate thing to ask considering the topic at hand, but I couldn't help asking the question.

She laughed. "Not many. Adam was too busy with school and sports. It was Will that was quite the player. He had a different girlfriend every month."

I could see that. "So why would they suspect him? High school was twenty years ago."

"Apparently they kept up with each other on social media, but they hadn't seen each other in person since high school—until two nights ago."

"The night she was murdered."

"Right. And he was the last person to see her ... except the person who killed her of course," she added quickly.

"Whoa." I sat back in my chair. I'd thought we'd heard the last of Mila's death because we had no connection to it, but now Adam's older brother was suspected of killing her. What were the odds? Of course, with my bad luck for finding bodies and getting entangled in murder investigations, I should have known better.

"Did he have any idea who could have killed her?" A thought occurred to me. "Why was he meeting her at night anyway? Your mom said he was out half the night."

Desi grimaced. "He said it was completely innocent— they met by accident at the pub downtown and shared a few drinks together."

"Do you think he's telling the truth?" I bit into my sandwich, but struggled to swallow it, my appetite suddenly diminished.

"I don't know. Things seem pretty rocky between him and Tania." She stared at my latte. "I need some coffee." She pushed herself up from her chair and came back a few minutes later with a tall mug of creamy coffee. Sipping it, she said, "Ah, that's better. After Will came in and told me what was going on, my mind's been a mess."

"No wonder." My own brain was spinning from the news. It was so loud in there that I could barely hear my own thoughts. "Do you think it was a coincidence that he happened to meet an old flame at the pub? Or did they have plans?"

"I don't know, but what difference does it make? He's still a suspect." She tapped the top of the mug's handle with her thumb.

"It seems like if it were a chance meeting, he wouldn't have had much of a reason to kill her. If it was something planned, they may have had more of a relationship than he's letting on and, therefore, more motive."

"You don't seriously think my brother could have killed her, do you?" She narrowed her eyes at me.

Did I? I didn't know Will very well, but although I could easily picture him fooling around on his wife, I'd never thought of him as the murderous type. But then again, you never really knew. I'd been surprised in the past.

I caught the person at the table next to us listening and gave them a look. They had the good grace to blush and get up from their table. "No, I guess not. But if the police do ..."

"We have to figure out what really happened to Mila. We saw her body before anyone else did. Think. Is there anything that struck you as odd about her death?"

"Uh, other than the fact that someone killed a seemingly nice woman?"

She glared at me.

"Ok, ok." I thought back to seeing her body. The image of her hanging from the Christmas lights would haunt me forever. "Her outfit."

"What about it?"

"She was wearing dress pants and a nice shirt. With heels. Not exactly appropriate for climbing up on the roof. I don't think she'd planned to be climbing any ladders."

"So what was she doing up there so late at night?" Desi pondered.

"The receptionist said she was a perfectionist and had complained about the lights. She probably went back there after she and Will hung out at the pub."

"If that's true, then whoever it was must have been watching her and waiting for the perfect opportunity to move the ladder out from underneath her."

"Yeah. So if it wasn't Will, it must have been someone from the retirement home, right? If she went inside the building first, someone could have seen her there."

"Unless it was ..." Desi stopped. "I hate to say it, but what if Tania killed her? If you're right and there was more to the relationship between Will and Mila, maybe Tania knew."

"You just accused our sister-in-law of murder." My stomach rolled. I didn't like Tania much, but a murderer?

"I know," she said quietly. "But we can't rule it out and I'm sure the police won't either."

"I hope the girls don't find out about all of this." Although my mother-in-law thought that they weren't affected by their parents' marital issues, I had a sneaking suspicion that very little got past my nieces. They were curious and intelligent kids who were into everything.

"I'm sure once my mom finds out, she'll do everything in her power to keep it from them."

"Wait, Will hasn't told your mom yet?" My hand flew out, jostling the coffee cup and splashing a drop of liquid on the table.

She shook her head. "He said he didn't want to worry her with her heart problems. If the police investigation progresses, then he'll say something."

Great. So now I had to keep this huge secret quiet from my mother-in-law—who I saw practically every day. I dabbed at the spilled coffee with a paper napkin.

"Desi, do you remember what Delilah said when we were outside with her?"

"No, why? What did she say?"

"Right before the boys showed up, she made some comment about the police not doing much about the other things that have happened around there. What do you think she meant by that?"

She stood from the table and collected her cup. "I don't know, but I think we need to find out. I'll pick you up tomorrow at eleven and we can stop in at the retirement home to talk to her before we start our shift at the historical homes tour, ok?"

I hesitated. Did I really want to get into another murder investigation? I caught sight of the determination on Desi's face. Her brother's freedom and reputation was at stake.

"Eleven sounds good. It will be nice to check on Delilah."

She nodded.

A line had formed again and Desi returned to the counter to help fill orders. I watched her work, still trying to process the news that Will was a murder suspect and I had to keep the secret from his mother. I'd come to the café for lunch and a break from work, but suddenly, immersing myself in a pile of work sounded like a breath of fresh air.

6

---

*D*esi pulled up to the curb outside of my house at ten minutes after eleven and rolled down her window. "Sorry," she called out to me. "Lina started crying at the same time as Anthony jumped off the couch and banged his ear against the coffee table. I had to help Tomàs get him cleaned up and both of them calmed down."

I stood from where I'd been sitting on the porch steps. "No problem. We should still have plenty of time to check on Delilah before we're due at the historic homes tour at twelve thirty."

I got into the passenger seat of her minivan and buckled up. A glowing orange light on the dashboard caught my eye. "Desi, why is the check engine light lit up?"

She scoffed. "Oh, it comes on sometimes. We haven't figured out what's wrong with it yet, but the car seems to run fine. It's probably just a loose connection in the dash or something. Don't worry about it."

It did run fine—until we were two miles away from home and two miles away from the retirement home. More lights flashed on the dashboard and the car made an ominous whirring sound.

Desi maneuvered the car to the shoulder.

"Should we worry about the check engine light now?" I asked dryly.

She shot an icy death glare at me. "It's not funny."

"Ok, ok. Do we want to wait for a tow truck to come and get your car, or do we want to walk to the tour? It's not that far away." I checked my watch. "I don't think we'll have time to see Delilah now, no matter what we do."

"I'll call Tomàs to come and get us and have the car towed to the shop. It's probably time for a professional to look at it."

"Probably," I agreed.

She called Tomàs and then hung up after speaking with him. "He'll be here in about thirty minutes. He has to get both kids into the car first and Lina's asleep in her crib at the moment so he has to wake her up."

I looked outside. "At least we aren't on a busy street. That's one good thing."

"Yeah, one good thing." She reclined her seat a bit more. "I really wanted to talk with Delilah though to find out what she was talking about."

"Maybe we'll have time to talk with her afterward. We can walk to Ericksville Heights from whichever home we end up being the tour guides for. It's not that far away from the houses on the tour. In fact, your mom should find out if they'll allow the retirement home to be a part of the tour next year. All of those stories Delilah told us about the home's history were fascinating."

"I can mention it to her." Desi looked out the window. "I can't believe I let Mom talk us into this. I'm happy to help out the Historical Society and all, but I'm crunched for time with Christmas coming up."

"Me too. My sister decided last minute to visit us for Christmas and I don't have a present for her. We don't usually exchange gifts, but it feels weird to have everyone else opening presents on Christmas Day and not have anything for her to open."

"Well, what does she like? Clothes? Perfume? Jewelry?" Desi asked.

"None of the above." I frowned. Becky was impossible to buy for. "Maybe some sort of hiking gear? She loves hiking, but she's not much for material things."

"Maybe a gift card?" Desi asked, tapping her chin.

"Maybe. Whatever it is, I need to figure it out soon." Flashing lights appeared from behind us and pulled ahead of our car on the shoulder.

"At least the tow truck is here," I said. "Whenever I call them, it takes hours."

She smiled smugly at me. "The police department uses this company sometimes, so they know Tomàs."

We stepped out of the car and Desi greeted the tow truck driver, signed something on his sheet, and gave him the keys. He loaded up the car and swung it off of the shoulder.

"She looks so sad," Desi said, staring at her minivan.

I patted her on the shoulder. "I'm sure she'll be fine. But where's Tomàs? It's been forty minutes already."

As if on cue, Tomàs pulled up in his SUV. Desi hopped into the passenger seat and I wedged myself in between the two car seats. A few minutes later, we were at the staging area for the historic homes tour. The Ericksville Heights Retirement Home was visible a short distance up the hill, the grand dame watching over all the other houses along the bluff.

"Give me a call when you want me to pick you up," he said.

"We will. Thank you!" I said.

He left and Desi and I made our way toward the small group gathered on the lawn of a three-story home from the early 1900s. The style of this home was similar to that of the retirement home, but thankfully, the Christmas lights that had been hung from this one were unsullied by a body hanging from them.

"I hope we get to be the guides at some really cool old house," I said. "After hearing Delilah's stories about early Ericksville, I'd love to see the inside of some of these."

"We did get to see Angela's house," Desi reminded me.

"Yeah, but I was too busy trying to investigate a murder to pay any attention to it." I looked in the direction of Angela's house, about a block down the hill. Her house, with its Gothic influences, was spookily beautiful, but the memory of the body we'd found in her storage shed—not so much.

The leader of the historic homes tour, a woman in her early seventies with tight graying curls, consulted her clipboard, calling off names and handing out assignments.

"Do you know her?" I asked Desi.

She nodded. "That's Tilly. She's been a member of the Ericksville Historical Society forever. I remember her coming over to the house when I was a little kid." She smiled. "She brought us chocolate bunnies at Easter one year."

I looked at Tilly. What would it be like to live in a town with so many memories? I'd never regretted moving to Adam's hometown after we were married, but there was a part of me that wondered what it would have been like to have our kids grow up in Coeur D'Alene where my parents had been teachers at the local schools. However, the good thing about moving away from Idaho was that when I returned there to visit my parents, a pleasant wave of nostalgia hit me every time I came back.

"Desi Torres and Jill Andrews," she finally called out.

"We're here." Desi stepped forward.

"Great. It's nice seeing you again, Desi. You've been so busy, we haven't seen you around much at the Historical Society." She peered at Desi, but although her words could have indicated she was subtly chiding Desi, she appeared to be sincere. "It's too bad your mother wasn't able to join us, but I know how busy she is at the Boathouse during the holidays. I'm really happy you're here to help." She beamed at us and handed a sheet of paper to Desi. "Here is your assignment. Thank you for helping make this day a success." She scurried off down the hill, presumably to the house where she was playing tour guide.

I rubbed my hands together. "So where do we get to go? This is so exciting." The row of elegant mansions along the cliff was one of my favorite things about Ericksville. How had I never thought to take advantage of the historic homes tour in the past so I could catch a glimpse of the insides of them?

Because of the time commitment, I hadn't been too sure about this when Beth had roped me into helping. She'd wanted to help out herself, but she had an event going on at the Boathouse and couldn't participate. Although she'd assured me that it would be fun, I'd had my doubts until we were standing on the green lawn of the massive old estate.

"You're not going to believe this." Desi looked up from the sheet of paper she'd been given.

"What is it? We're not guides for Angela's house, are

we?" It would shock me if Angela was participating in the tour, as she valued her privacy.

She handed me the piece of paper wordlessly.

I skimmed it. "The Dunlop house?"

"Keep reading."

The address of the house meant nothing to me, but my eyes stopped when I reached the owner's name.

"Nancy Davenport? There has to be some sort of mistake."

"Nope. No mistake. We're going to be spending the next two hours showing people around Nancy's house."

7

We showed up on Nancy's doorstep a few minutes later, neither of us wanting to ring the bell.

"You do it," I whispered to Desi.

She rolled her eyes and pressed the button. Inside, a set of chimes played an excessively long song to alert the residents that someone was at the door.

"Who is it?" Nancy called out from behind the door.

"We're here for the historic homes tour," Desi answered.

Nancy flung open the door with a smile, which slipped off as soon as she saw who was on her porch. "I thought you said you were here for the tour."

I sighed. "We are. Desi and I were assigned to be the tour guides for your house."

She eyed us, as if trying to decide whether or not we were telling the truth. Her final decision must have been that we weren't there for nefarious purposes, because she said, "Fine. Come in, come in. Don't you know better than to stand in the doorway letting the cold air in?"

I could tell already that this was not going to be as fun as I'd imagined.

"You have a beautiful house, Nancy," Desi said. "I didn't realize you lived up on the bluffs." She turned her gaze up to the two-story high ceiling in the entry hall and a grand spiral staircase.

"Yes," Nancy said tightly. "My family has lived here since Ericksville was settled."

"Oh, wow. That's great. It must be so nice to live somewhere that has so much of your family's history." I smiled at her, hoping to melt her icy demeanor.

She regarded me with suspicion. "It is nice." She turned abruptly and motioned to the room off of the entry. "Now, if you're going to be giving tours, let me show you around the place." She moved quickly from room to room, showing us a parlor full of antiques, including a horsehair sofa and an upright piano and a library filled with old books. We climbed up the winding oak staircase to the second floor.

"These are my children's rooms. You can let people go into the entrance to each, but please don't let them touch anything. The same goes for the master bedroom."

We walked into a magnificent master bedroom with a wide-open vista of Puget Sound. A king-sized bed was pushed up against one wall and a set of arm chairs had been positioned in front of the windows. I caught a glimpse of a bathroom with marble and gold fixtures before Nancy closed the door.

I completely forgot where I was and walked to the window as if in a trance to take in the view. "This is amazing." The blue-gray water glittered like a sheet of broken glass in front of us, so close that I felt as though I could touch it. Willowby Island soared above the water and, even from this distance, I could just make out houses along its shores.

"Please don't touch the windows." Nancy sniffed. "I don't want fingerprints on the glass."

I turned away from the window and Desi smirked at me from behind Nancy's back. "I'm sorry. I was just admiring the view."

Nancy spun around without a word and strode off, evidently expecting us to follow her. We continued down a back staircase, into a large kitchen with traditional black and white squares on the floor. She pushed open a door at the back of the kitchen.

"This is the butler's pantry."

"Is there a door behind there?" I pointed to an antique armoire that almost completely concealed a wooden door in the pantry.

She stared at it as though she'd forgotten it was there. "Yes. That goes to the basement." She shivered. "We don't have any reason to go downstairs, so we keep it closed up. I don't want the kids playing down there."

Nancy continued on down the first floor hallway toward the front door, reeling off the names of the rooms and briefly tapping on a closed door as she went by. "This is my office. Don't open the door."

The place was like a maze and I wasn't sure how I was going to guide people through it. At the front door, Nancy shoved a map of the rooms and a small description of each at Desi and me. "I trust this will be enough. I have an appointment I need to go to. Remember, don't let anyone touch anything." She eyed us again. "I hate leaving you two alone in my house, but I don't really have a choice."

"We'll be careful with everything," Desi said sweetly. "Thank you for allowing your home to be on the tour."

When she'd roared out of the driveway, we both breathed sighs of relief.

"How clear are you on where everything is in the house?" I asked.

"Not very." She glanced toward the street, where a couple had just turned off of the main sidewalk and onto the walkway to the house. "We'd better get up to speed quickly though."

I scanned the map, trying to commit things to memory before I looked like an idiot to everyone touring Nancy's mansion.

"Hello," Desi said, greeting the man and woman, who looked to be in their sixties. "Thanks for visiting the Dunlop house. I'm Desi and I'll be your guide today." She read the information about the house off of the piece of paper and the couple followed her inside, leaving me alone on the porch.

Too soon, a group of women appeared, all wearing red hats. They stopped outside of the house and attempted to take a group photo of themselves. After one of them almost dropped her phone, I stepped in.

"Do you want me to take one?"

They nodded enthusiastically.

"That would be wonderful, dear." A woman with short, straight gray hair handed me her phone to take the picture. I snapped a shot and gave it back to them.

"I'm Jill, and I'll be your guide today." I smiled at them. "You'll have to bear with me though. This is my first tour of the day."

"Oh, honey, I'm sure you'll be great at it," another woman said. Her friends murmured words of encouragement.

I led them into the house and showed them around.

They oohed and aahed over the view upstairs. By the time we headed down through the first floor pantry, I was feeling pretty good about things. At the front door, they thanked me for my time and went on their way.

Desi wasn't in the entry hallway, so she must have already taken another group in. Judging by the line that had formed in the last ten minutes, we would be busy. We continued taking groups through the house for the next two hours.

I introduced myself to a group of people who were next in line, including a woman and her little girl, who wore an adorable blue dress and looked to be about four. I brought them inside the house and they admired the parlor and library, then toured the upstairs. I was finishing my final speech about the kitchen and pantry when the little girl tugged on her mother's arm.

"Mommy," she said in a loud voice. "I have to go potty."

Her mother leaned down. "Can you wait until we get home?"

"No." A panicked expression appeared on the little girl's face. "I have to go now."

The mother looked at me apologetically. "Do you think the owner of the house would mind if my daughter uses the bathroom? I'm afraid she'll have an accident if she doesn't go soon."

A potty accident in Nancy's house would be even worse than fingerprints. Plus, Nancy had a bunch of kids and worked at a preschool, so she wouldn't mind, right? I glanced at the girl, who was now doing the potty dance. The rest of the group had exited the house, so I jutted my thumb toward the back hallway.

"I'm sure they wouldn't mind. Let's see where it is." I walked down the hallway behind the kitchen, but found no bathroom, only the broom closet and a sterile-looking guest bedroom. There were only two rooms left. One was Nancy's office and I assumed the other was the bathroom. I crossed my fingers that I'd open the correct room.

I turned the doorknob and peeked in. Some light shone through the windows, illuminating a room filled with—cats. Cats?

"Mommy, I have to go NOW!"

I left the room behind and hurriedly opened the last door, revealing a modern bathroom. The girl ran inside and sat down on the toilet before her mother could even close the door. I stepped back to give her privacy and went back to Nancy's office to close the door.

Before I shut it, I couldn't help but look in the room for longer. I'd already opened Pandora's box, so why not see it fully?

There was a nice white desk along one wall, but the rest of Nancy's office was filled with everything cat related. A cat clock hung from the wall, its tail swishing back and forth with each passing second. Pictures of cats of all colors and varieties hung from the walls and a rug in the shape of a big orange cat covered a quarter of the floor.

Something moved, startling me until I realized what it was. A real cat sat on a plush purple pillow on the windowsill. I was worried that she'd try to escape, but she only glanced at me with a lazy expression and then turned back to the window.

"Jill?" Desi called out. "Where are you?"

"Down the hall," I answered. The door to the bathroom was still closed.

Desi came up behind me. "Hey, isn't that Nancy's office?"

"Yup." I pushed the door open further. "Check it out."

Desi's eyes widened as she took in the catdom. "Whoa."

"No kidding. No wonder she didn't want us to see it. Nancy is the crazy cat lady."

Desi smirked. "Well, we always knew about the crazy part, but this?" She poked her head in further and the fluffy white cat on the windowsill stretched out her paw at us. Before we knew it, she'd jumped down and was heading toward the open door.

"Shut it," I yelled.

Desi slammed the door just in time. We both leaned back against the wall.

"That was close," I said, my heart rate slowly returning to normal.

"Yeah. Too close," Desi said. "Nancy would kill us if we let her cat out." She looked at me. "What were you doing in there anyway?"

The bathroom door opened, and the woman and little girl came out. "Thanks so much for letting her use the bathroom."

"No problem. Enjoy the rest of the tour." I turned to Desi. "I was trying to find the bathroom, and I accidentally opened the wrong door." I laughed. "But now I'm kind of glad I did. Who would have thought?"

"We can never mention this to anyone," Desi said as she tried to keep a straight face.

I zipped my fingers across my lips. "I'm certainly not telling anyone. Hey, do we have more groups to lead through?"

"There wasn't anyone when I came back down from my last tour." She held up her watch to show me the time. "I think the homes tour is almost officially over."

"Thank goodness."

I heard a car in the driveway, and we moved out of the hallway, far away from the cat room.

Nancy entered the house, eyeing everything. As far as I knew, nothing was out of place. "I trust things went fine?"

"Yes. Perfectly." Desi smiled at her. "People were very complimentary about your house."

"Good." She looked at us if as if wondering why we were still there.

I took the hint and grabbed Desi's arm. "Thanks so much for having your house on the tour."

Desi and I walked out of the house and made it to the sidewalk before we both broke out into a fit of giggles.

"Did you see that clock? And the rug?" I asked.

She nodded. "I'd never have guessed that prim and proper Nancy would have a room in her house devoted to cats."

"Me neither. I'm so glad that the preschool isn't in session until after the new year. I'm happy to have a break from Nancy, but also so that I won't accidentally tell her that I know about her cat room." I shook my head and smiled. "It's such a juicy secret." I looked up the hill toward the retirement home. "Do you still want to check on Delilah?"

"I think we should."

"Me too."

8

The mood at the Ericksville Heights Retirement Home was much more somber than when we'd been there a few days ago with the preschool class. Desi and I checked in at the front desk and they told us that we could find Delilah in the Great Room, which turned out to be a large space with a giant river rock fireplace. Delilah was sitting near the fire, with an afghan over her lap.

When we neared her, she glanced at us, but didn't say anything, just turned back around to stare at the fire.

Desi put her hand on her shoulder. "Delilah, are you feeling ok?"

Delilah nodded. "I'm fine. Just a bit tired today."

She looked as though she'd aged five years since we last saw her. Her skin was crepey and her eyes dull, as though she hadn't been sleeping well.

We pulled up chairs near her.

"We thought we'd come and visit you because we were in the area for the historic homes tour," Desi said.

Sadness crossed Delilah's face. "Oh no, I missed the tour. I go every year, but I must not have written it down correctly on my calendar this year." She sighed. "Dates and times are starting to get away from me."

"That's ok," Desi said, trying to cheer her up. "It's the same houses every year, right? You've probably been in all of them already."

Delilah brightened. "You're right, dear. But still, I would have liked to support the Historical Society."

I thought a change of subject might be good. "How are things here? Did the police discover anything about Mila's death?"

Delilah shook her head. "No, they don't tell us anything."

Desi looked at me, then said, "You know my brother Will, right?"

She smiled. "Of course I remember Will. Always such a cheery kid. Isn't he a fancy doctor in Arizona now?"

"Normally, yes, he lives in Arizona. But he's up here with his family for Christmas."

"That's wonderful." She looked wistful. "Your mother must be so happy."

"She is." Desi paused. "But Will is a suspect in Mila's murder."

Delilah recoiled. "Excuse me?"

"He had drinks with her the night she died and is one of the last people to see her alive." Desi sighed loudly.

"I thought he was married?" Delilah asked.

"It's complicated," I said.

"Of course he didn't do it," Delilah said indignantly. "He wouldn't hurt a fly."

"Thanks for saying that," Desi said. "But until the real murderer is found, he's a suspect.

"Your poor mother. This must be devastating to her."

Desi squirmed a little. "She doesn't know yet. Will doesn't want to worry her."

She nodded approvingly. "Good for him."

I tried to steer the conversation back to Mila's death. "Have the police been around here after the day Mila was found?"

"No. Not that I know of." She gazed out the window toward the backyard. "And unfortunately, now that Mila isn't here, they've cancelled our Christmas party. We were all looking forward to it so much."

"I'm so sorry," Desi said. "Maybe that would have made things a little cheerier around here."

"I'm sorry too." I frowned. "Can't someone else take over organizing the Christmas party? Maybe Mila's assistant?"

"No, until they hire someone new, her assistant has too much on her plate with the regular events around here." She tilted her head up to me. "You're an event coordinator, aren't you?"

I nodded. "I am." I had a feeling I knew where this was going and I already felt bad.

"Do you think that you could manage the party? I bet they could pay you for your time." Hope was written across her face.

"I'm so sorry, but my time is completely booked until after Christmas."

Her face crumbled and I felt as though I'd slapped an old lady in the face.

"I wish there was something I could do to help. It sounds like Mila had a wonderful party planned for all of the residents."

"She always did make everything nice for us," she said sadly. "Ever since Mila passed, things haven't been the same. She was such a delightful woman."

"Does anyone have any theories about what happened to her?" I asked. I figured that in the close confines of the retirement home, gossip would run rampant and with all of those ideas converging, the residents might stumble upon the truth.

She looked around nervously. "I've heard some talk that it might be related to some of the other suspicious deaths around here."

I looked around the room at the half dozen senior citizens who were relaxing in the Great Room and leaned in closer to her. "Have there been some deaths that seemed out of the ordinary?"

Her chin bobbed up and down. "I think so. Lenny Landers was in good health and then they found him lying dead in his room one morning. The official response was that it was a heart attack, but you can't help but wonder because I've heard rumors that he'd fallen for some scam right before he died. The same thing happened to Albert Wendil. He was here one day, and gone the next." A tear slipped down her wrinkled cheek. "It's probably silly of me to say such things."

"I don't know. If you think something isn't right, it's probably not," Desi said. "Did anyone talk to the police about it?"

Delilah uttered a harsh laugh. "Sure, they came to take the report, but nobody's heard from them since. We told Mila there was something really wrong and she said she'd look into it." She looked at her lap.

"So what do you and the others think happened to those men?" I asked.

"I think that—" She stared at something in the back of the room for a moment and her eyes became unfocused. "I'm sorry, I'm very tired. I should go rest in my room."

I turned my attention to the back of the room where

she'd been looking, but saw nothing out of the ordinary. What had Delilah seen?

"Of course," Desi said sympathetically. "You've had a rough week. Jill and I completely understand."

I nodded. "We'll come see you another day, ok?" I'd developed a soft spot for the elderly woman as my own grandparents had died many years before.

Delilah nodded and slowly rose to her feet with the help of her walker. "Have a nice afternoon, girls." She walked off, pushing the walker in front of her. The colorful pink tennis balls attached to the walker's back legs swished along the hardwood floors as she walked down the hall toward her room.

"I feel so bad for her," Desi said. "Mom said Delilah doesn't have much family around here and that Mila's death has probably hit her hard."

"Yeah." I glanced at the back of the Great Room. "Did you notice that she was about to tell us something about the mysterious deaths and then she just stopped talking?"

"I did, but I assumed she was just tired." Desi cocked her head to the side. "Do you think something scared her away from telling us?"

I shrugged. "I don't know. She looked at something in the back of the room right before she stopped talking. By the time I turned to look, I didn't see anyone back there."

"Hmm." Desi scanned the room. "I don't see anything weird in here either, but it could have been someone that was only here briefly."

"But long enough to frighten Delilah." A sense of dread swirled around the pit of my stomach. I'd become fond of the kind old woman and the thought that anyone would intentionally frighten her made me ill.

"My spidey senses are telling me something isn't right

here." Desi stood. "I'm going to call Tomàs to come and pick us up, but if it's ok with you, I'd like for us to visit Delilah together again. Maybe next time she will feel comfortable enough to finish what she was saying."

"I definitely agree. Let's try to come back early next week, ok?"

Desi nodded. "And I'll talk to my mom about this." The corners of her mouth turned down. "I don't know if Will has told her yet about being a suspect though. I'll have to tread carefully until I know. But maybe she'll have an idea of what is bothering Delilah. They see each other every week at the Historical Society meetings, so maybe she can get something out of her that we couldn't."

She called Tomàs and he picked us up with their kids in the car. The ride back to my house was short, and I was soon back home where Adam and I hung out with the kids until bedtime. I tried to focus on my family, but thoughts of Ericksville Heights and Delilah kept running through my mind. What was bothering Delilah and how did it fit in with Mila's murder? I hated the thought of getting involved in another murder investigation, but like it or not, I seemed to have found myself smack in the middle of one.

9

*U*sually, I had our Christmas tree up just after Thanksgiving, but this year was different. It was December sixteenth, and I'd just asked Adam to pull it out of the storage above our garage. He wheeled the plastic storage container into the living room and Mikey ran to it with Ella toddling close on his heels.

"Can I help, Mommy?" he asked, his chubby fingers already trying to pry the lid off of the box.

I laughed. "Yes, you can both help." I moved Ella out of the way and Mikey helped me to remove the three parts of our fake Christmas tree from the box. When I was a kid, we always went to a Christmas tree farm as a family and cut down a live tree, but as an adult with children of our own, Adam and I had opted for the simplicity of a fake tree. However, I still missed the wonderful aroma of a fresh Christmas tree. Maybe the tree lot by the gas station had some tree branch swags left so our house would at least smell like Christmas.

Mikey positioned the base of the tree on top of the

green, red, and white tree skirt I'd placed on the floor near the fireplace.

"Here, Mommy?" He looked up at me with wide blue eyes, and a rush of love for him shot through me. Christmas had always been my favorite time of year, and seeing my kids experience the joy of the holiday made me even happier.

"Yes, honey. It looks wonderful." I set the second and third layers on top of it, then attempted to connect the lights. Even with the two ends pressed tightly together, the top two tiers wouldn't light.

"Do you want some help?" Adam asked as he came back into the room with a large green tub full of ornaments.

I sighed. "Yes. I hate trying to figure out if a bulb is loose, or what." On the plus side, at least with a fake, pre-lit tree, you didn't have to worry about the strings of lights getting tangled. Bile rose in my throat at the thought of finding Mila's body hanging in a sea of twisted lights.

I turned away from the tree while Adam tinkered with it and opened the box of ornaments. We'd banished all of our glass ornaments to the cushioned bottom of the bin and only used non-breakable ornaments since the kids were born. With Ella toddling around this year, it was especially important to make sure she couldn't get hurt on anything. The soft ornaments had the added benefit of not breaking when Fluffy, our cat, tried to climb into the tree and acciden-tally knocked ornaments off. She also had the odd habit of bringing us ornaments late at night as offerings while meowing her head off, and I didn't fancy the idea of step-ping on a glass ornament with bare feet.

"There," Adam said with a self-satisfied smile. "It's working now." He stepped back to allow us all room to view the tree. The multi-colored lights twinkled like stars in the sky and filled me with warmth.

I knelt down and wrapped my arms around Mikey and Ella. "Isn't it pretty?"

Mikey nodded solemnly and Ella stared at it in rapt wonder. Last year she'd been only a couple of months old, so she hadn't been able to experience many of our Christmas traditions, but I had a feeling she'd enjoy this year.

"Oh, honey, I forgot to tell you," Adam began. "A client contacted me yesterday and wants me to meet with them tomorrow morning."

"On Monday morning?" I glanced at the calendar. Preschool was on winter break until after New Year's. This time, considering Adam's declaration that he had to work, even the thought of two weeks without Nancy didn't bring me joy. "You're supposed to watch the kids tomorrow, remember? Mikey's on break from school and your mom and I are both busy at the Boathouse. We're booked solid with company Christmas parties this week."

"I know," he said. "Can't the babysitter watch them?"

"No." I counted to ten in my head. I'd already gone over all of this with him several times, but he never seemed to listen. "The university is on break too and she went home for the holidays."

"Oh." He picked up a cloth teddy bear ornament out of the box and hooked it on a tree branch. "So what are we going to do? This is an important meeting with a new client and it could lead to bigger things."

"I don't know." I grabbed a handful of ornaments and threw them on the tree with less care than normal.

"Hey," he said, gently stopping my hand as I dipped back into the box for more ornaments. "I'll figure it out, ok?"

I stared at him. "Who are you going to get to watch them at such short notice?" The holiday stress I felt was increasing, and now, even the task of decorating the tree was getting to me. Beside me, Mikey picked out a soft ornament and handed it to his sister, then helped her place it on a bottom branch. My heart melted a little seeing him be so good to her. I took a deep breath. "I'm sure you'll figure it out, but let me know if things don't work out. I can maybe rearrange some things in my schedule if I need to."

"Having new clients is a good thing, honey. We need my practice to start making money."

Guilt showered over me. He'd worked so hard to get his law practice up and running. I couldn't be upset that he had a client meeting. Besides, with all of the expenses associated with Christmas, he was right. We could use the money. Having a variable income was taking more getting used to than I'd thought it would.

Adam squeezed my shoulders. "Have faith in me—in us. I know we're still trying to figure out how things will fit together with all of the changes in our life, but we'll make it work."

I looked into his eyes, and he smiled at me.

"Ok," I said. I handed the kids some more ornaments and gave the angel tree topper to Adam.

While he worked on getting the small light in it hooked up to the rest of the lights, we finished decorating the tree. Adam flicked a switch on the angel, and we all stepped back to admire the tree with the glowing angel atop it.

"It's beautiful," I said, entranced. All of the hope that the season usually held flooded over me. There were so many things stressing me out right now—my family's impending visit, Mila's murder, and the upcoming parties I would be coordinating at the Boathouse. Somehow, though, I knew that everything would work out.

That night, after the kids were in bed, there was a knock at the door. Adam and I had been relaxing together in front of the TV on the couch. We exchanged glances.

"Were you expecting someone?" he asked.

"Nope."

He got up and went over to the door, checking to see who it was through the peephole, then threw it open.

"Hey." Will stood on our porch with his hands in his pockets. "Can I come in?"

Adam checked with me first, and I nodded.

"Hi, Will. Come in." I stood from the couch and motioned for him to come and sit at the dining room table. "Sit down and I'll make a pot of coffee."

He stepped inside and removed his boots. "Thanks."

When the three of us were seated around the table with cups of coffee and an open bag of Oreos, I said, "I'm surprised to see you tonight. I wouldn't have thought Beth would let you out of her sight." I smiled. "She's so thrilled to have you back home, even for a short time."

He wrapped his hands around his coffee mug. "I know. I thought I'd see if you guys had time to chat. I needed some time away from Mom and Dad, and the girls are already in bed."

"What's going on?" Adam asked. "Jill told me about what happened with Mila. I'm sorry for your loss. She was always a sweet girl."

"Thanks." He sipped his coffee. "The only contact we'd really had in twenty years was a few friendly messages on social media and then I ran into her at the pub that night."

"So why do the police consider you a suspect in the murder investigation?"

He shrugged. "That's actually the reason I wanted to talk to the two of you." He looked at me. "Mom's told me about some of the murders you helped to solve. I was hoping that if I talked with you about that night that you might see something that I'm missing. The police said I was the last known person to see her alive."

"Were you?" I asked.

"I'm sure someone at the retirement home must have seen her that night. She went in a side door, but still."

"So you were there that night? At Ericksville Heights?" Adam peered at him. "If it was just a few drinks, why were you at her workplace? Help me to understand."

Will pushed his chair back and ran his fingers through his hair. "The whole time we were at the pub, she seemed anxious about something. Then she was going on and on about the Christmas tree lights being crooked. I don't remember her being quite so worried about everything when she was a teenager."

"Life has a tendency to do that to you," I said. "But why were you at the home?"

"She said she had some work she'd forgotten to do earlier and that she was going to walk over there from the pub we were at in downtown Ericksville. She said she'd call a ride service to get home from there when she was done. It was late at night and even here, I didn't think it was a good idea for her to be out alone at night. I guess I had a reason to be concerned." His eyes misted over. "I walked with her to Ericksville Heights and I watched her go in the side door. That was the last I saw of her."

"So she never told you she was going to fix the Christmas lights?"

"No," he said sharply. "I would have insisted that she go straight home if I'd known that she planned to go up on the roof wearing heels."

I thought about the red heels I'd tripped over. If she'd had a few drinks, she probably hadn't been in a good state of mind to hear someone following her.

He gazed at me expectantly. "So, was there anything of use in what I said?"

I think he'd expected me to work miracles. "It's not like some parlor game where I can hear a narrative and figure out the culprit."

"But you believe me, right?" His eyes moved between Adam and me.

"Of course we do," Adam said. "Right, Jill?"

I looked directly into Will's eyes. They were full of pain, but not deceit. "I believe you."

"Thank you." He was quiet for a moment. "I don't want to tell Mom though, so can the two of you keep quiet about it? She doesn't need more stress."

"I won't tell her," Adam said. "But you know she's going to find out."

"I know. Maybe by that time I'll be cleared by the police. They have to realize I'm innocent at some point."

He still hadn't told Beth. My heart sank. His voice was so earnest and a little innocent. He appeared to have little clue of how serious the situation was. "I'm sure they will, but first they need to be looking for other suspects. Right now, the police seem to only be focusing on you."

"You found her body," Will said. "Do you know anything that might help the police discover the real killer?"

"Not at the moment." I thought it best to not mention

Delilah's suspicions about the other recent deaths at the retirement home until we knew something conclusively about them. I hastily added, "But I can ask around a little."

Adam frowned. "I don't want you getting involved in this. It could be dangerous."

Will's face fell. "I wouldn't want you to do anything that could hurt you. It's better if we leave this to the police."

"I won't do anything to raise suspicion. I may ask a few questions at the retirement home, but I'll leave the actual investigation up to the police. Ok?" I peered into Adam's face. He didn't look like he believed me.

"Please be careful." His face was etched with concern.

I patted his hand. "I will."

Will cleared his throat and stood from the table. "Well, thanks. I really appreciate the talk. I'd better get back home before Mom decides I've broken curfew."

Adam laughed. "I'm glad we had a chance to talk too." He paused for a moment and looked at me, then back to his brother. "Hey, Will—remember how you wanted for you and the girls to spend more time with our kids?"

I saw where this was going and wondered how Will would react.

"Yeah, why?" Will asked.

"Jill and I need someone to babysit the kids tomorrow. Our babysitter's out of town and everyone else is busy. Would you mind watching them over at Mom and Dad's house tomorrow morning? It would only be for a few hours." Adam rubbed his thumb idly along the back of the chair.

Will's face broke out into a smile. "I'd love to, and I'm sure the girls will be happy to see their cousins too. You can drop them off in the morning."

"Thank you so much," I said. "We really appreciate this."

"No problem. That's what family is for." He grinned. "Well, I'd better get going, but I'm looking forward to seeing the munchkins tomorrow morning."

"See you tomorrow," Adam said.

"Bye, Will." I was surprised at Will's reaction when Adam asked him to babysit. The Will I'd known in the past hadn't been that involved with his own kids, much less happy to babysit someone else's kids. Maybe he had changed over the years.

Will left and we closed the door behind him.

"I'm bushed, honey," Adam said. "I think I'm going to head to bed."

I was still on a caffeine high and didn't think I'd get to sleep any time soon. "I'm going to load the dishwasher so it can run tonight. I'll be up in a little bit."

"Night."

When he left, I placed our coffee mugs in the dishwasher and rinsed off the other dirty dishes before loading them in too. The familiar task gave me an opportunity to think without anyone else around. I believed Will when he said he hadn't killed Mila and that he'd watched her until she was safely inside the retirement home. So, whoever was responsible had almost certainly been associated with Ericksville Heights, but who? Will had said that Mila seemed anxious about something at work, but what had made her so upset?

10

The next morning, I dropped Ella and Mikey off with Will. I didn't know how well the day would go with taking care of his own girls too, but I didn't have much of a choice and it would be nice for them to get to know their uncle and cousins better.

I spent the morning working on the Pearson Company Christmas party, which was scheduled for the next Sunday evening and was the biggest event on my list. I'd talked to Lizzie, our catering manager, about the increased guest count and made arrangements for more round tables in the main room, but there was still much to do. When I'd called to tell them about striking out with the reindeer, they'd asked for the servers to be dressed as Santa's elves and for us to provide activities for the children, so I was scrambling to grant those requests.

My desk phone rang with an internal call. Why was Beth calling me from her office just down the hall?

"Hey, Jill, can you come down here for a moment?"

"Of course. I'll be there in a minute." I hung up, still not sure what was going on. Beth rarely called me when we were both at the Boathouse, instead choosing to walk to my office to get in contact with me.

I knocked on her open office door to alert her that I was there and entered the room.

"Have a seat," Beth said, looking up from a pile of papers. Her face was drawn and she was fidgeting with the edge of a piece of paper.

"What is it?" I perched on the edge of the seat, too nervous to get comfortable.

"I just got a phone call from Chas Pearson that the Pearson Christmas party has been cancelled." She folded her hands in front of her on the desk. "I'm sorry, Jill. I know you've put a lot of work into it."

Her words slammed into me. I'd been working on the party for the last few months, trying to make it perfect for one of our biggest clients.

"Why?" I managed to croak out. "Harry Pearson was so excited about making it perfect for his employees."

She sighed. "I'm sorry, honey, but Harry Pearson died."

I sat back in my chair. "He died? I just saw him a few weeks ago."

"His son Chas called and said that his father's health had been in decline and that he'd been living at Ericksville Heights for a couple of months."

"I never saw him there. I wish I'd known. I would have tried to visit him when I stopped by to see Delilah. He was a nice old man."

"I'm sure he was." She gave me a small smile. "Apparently his son has decided to close the business down effective immediately, and with no employees, there's no need for a holiday party."

My jaw dropped. "Right before Christmas?"

She looked at me sadly. "Sometimes it happens. On the

bright side, they've already paid their fifty percent deposit, so we shouldn't be out much money, but I feel badly that you've worked so hard on it."

I sat back in the chair. We'd had clients cancel events on us before, but they were usually not cancelled at the last minute and not ones where I'd already invested so much of my life in their event. And those poor employees, getting laid off right before Christmas. I may have lost hours of my time, but they were losing their livelihood.

"Did Chas say why they were closing?" I asked.

"No. He didn't volunteer the information, and I didn't ask." She moved some papers around on her desk. "All he said was that they'd need to cancel the event because the business was closing. With a quick closure like that, I'd assume there were financial problems, but I don't know for sure. At least we were already paid."

"Yeah, I guess." I stood from the chair. "Is there anything else I should do for the event?"

"You'll need to cancel anything we can and notify the staff that we may not have an event on Sunday night. There's a small balance on the account, but we'll just write that off instead of trying to get the money from them." She ran her fingers through her hair. "I hate doing this to our staff too. I'll try to see if I can drum up some business for Sunday night to make up for the loss of the event, but it's such short notice."

"I'll take care of cancelling everything." I walked back to my office, lost in thought. Not having the big event bearing down on me had lifted a weight from my shoulders, but I mourned the loss of all of those hours of work—hours I could have spent with my family instead.

To take my mind off of the event cancellation, I left the building to get some fresh air and walked over to the Beans-Talk Café.

It wasn't too busy at this time of the morning, so Desi served me herself.

"How's it going?" She peered at me. "You look like someone died." She sucked in her breath. "Did someone die?"

I bit my lip and averted my eyes.

Her eyes widened. "Oh no, who died?"

"Harry Pearson, the owner of the Pearson Company. I was planning their big Christmas party and his son just cancelled it. Beth said they closed their whole business."

"Oh!" she said. "I didn't know you were working on a party for them. Hold on." She ran into the back room and returned, holding a newspaper. She thrust the folded-up newspaper at me. "I was reading about it this morning. Look at the headline."

I looked at the front page of the paper, my eyes settling on a headline at the bottom of the paper. *Local business owner dies. Employees find doors shuttered.*

"What happened?" I murmured out loud.

She stabbed a finger at the paper. "Harry Pearson died at the retirement home on Saturday night and his son shut down the company before his father was even in the ground."

Saturday night? Desi and I had been at Ericksville Heights on Saturday. If I'd known he was ill, I would have liked to have visited him. Something occurred to me.

"Do you think this has to do with what Delilah said? About there being suspicious deaths at the retirement home?"

Desi shook her head. "He was eighty-eight. It was probably natural causes. But can you believe his son shuttered the company? I can't imagine going in to work and finding the doors locked and my job gone. And right before Christmas! Those poor people."

"No kidding." I skimmed the rest of the article. "What are the employees going to do?"

"I don't know. It doesn't sound like they'll get severance or anything, but they should get unemployment benefits."

"Sheesh. That's just so wrong." I closed up the newspaper. I almost wished I could still have the Christmas party for the company, but it would be expensive for us at the Boathouse and I didn't think they'd want a reminder that they were no longer employed by the Pearson Company.

Usually the thought of a Christmas party made me happy, but with this one cancelled because of a company shutdown and the retirement home party being cancelled because of Mila's death, it seemed to bring too much sadness for the season. I left the BeansTalk with a latte in a to-go cup and decided to walk the beach for a while to work out some of my melancholy.

Walking on the beach worked, and I returned to work at the Boathouse with a much clearer head. When I got back to my office, I located anything related to the Pearson Company Christmas party, including my revamped binder, and filed it away in a box that I'd move to the storage room. With that off my desk, I moved on to other projects.

At quitting time, I stopped in at Beth's office. She was still tapping away at her computer and sipping from a cup of coffee.

"I'm leaving now. Did you need me for anything else?" I leaned against the doorframe.

She looked up at me. "Nope, I'm good. I'm going home soon too."

I felt her eyes on my face.

"You look upset," she observed. "Is it about the party?"

Maybe I wasn't as clear-headed as I'd thought.

"I feel bad for all those people that lost their jobs so close to Christmas and for the residents at the retirement home because their recreation director was killed. Now they don't get a Christmas party because she was in charge of planning it. It doesn't seem fair." I sighed.

She regarded me for a moment. "I can't do anything about the company shutting down, but I have an idea. Why don't you organize the Christmas party for the retirement home?"

"Have you been talking to Delilah?"

"No, why?" She smiled. "Did she ask you to help?"

"Yeah, but I had to turn her down because I had so much to do with the Pearson party."

"Well, maybe this was a blessing in disguise." Beth shut her computer off and stood. "Now that the party is cancelled, you can help out Delilah. If you'd like to use work hours for it, I'm happy to pay you for your time. I know it would mean a lot to her and the other residents."

A glimmer of hope entered my body. She was right. I couldn't change any of the bad things that were happening around me, but this was something I could do.

She snapped her fingers. "I'll give her a call. Hold on." She dialed a number.

"Hi, Delilah, it's Beth Andrews." Delilah must have said something because Beth smiled and said, "Uh huh." She was quiet for a moment, then said, "I was just talking with my daughter-in-law, Jill, and she mentioned that your Christmas party had been cancelled because of the recreation director's death. We've had a cancellation here at the Boathouse, and she's available to help out with your party if the managers of the retirement home are interested." She was quiet. "Ok, great. I'll see you next week at the Historical Society meeting."

She hung up and turned to me. "Delilah said she'll talk to them about having you help. She's pretty sure they'll say yes because the residents are up in arms about not having the annual party."

"I'll stop by and talk to them tomorrow about the party. Maybe Mila already had some things in the works before she died and I can just follow her plans."

Beth shrugged. "Maybe. But whatever the case may be, I know you'll do a great job." She beamed at me. "I've trained you well."

I laughed. "I suppose you have."

We walked out of the Boathouse together and got into our cars. I appreciated Beth's faith in my abilities. My life would be vastly different if I had a relationship with her that was as bad as the one between her and Tania. Although I was upset by the cancellation of the Pearson Company's Christmas party, I was looking forward to helping Delilah and the other residents at Ericksville Heights with their party. I'd felt awful to not be able to help her before, and maybe this was exactly what I needed to get back into the holiday spirit.

11

When I walked into the retirement home the next morning, the receptionist greeted me and said, "If you're looking for Delilah, she's in the Great Room. That's where she spends most of her time."

"Thank you." I continued to the Great Room, quickly spotting Delilah at a table for two near the window. While some of the other residents had games or books in front of them, she had none, but was watching something intently outside of the window. Near the fireplace, I overheard a woman asking a nurse if she'd light the fire. A look of panic filled the nurse's face, and she rapidly twisted a wedding ring on her finger but quickly recovered and told the woman that she'd send someone by to take care of it. The resident wasn't happy and stomped off to the back of the room. Apparently there was more drama at a retirement home than one would expect. I shifted my attention to the reason I'd come.

"Hi, Delilah." I didn't want to startle her, so I tried to make some noise by shuffling my feet as I approached her.

She turned to me, and a wide smile spread across her face. "Jill. I'm so happy you're here."

"Me too." I realized that I really was very happy to be there and to be able to use my newfound organizational talents to create a special event for her and her fellow residents. "The woman at the front desk told me I could find you in here. Were you looking at something special outside?"

She pointed at the window. "Do you see that tree over there?"

I followed her finger to a large tree at the far side of the property. "Yes, I see it."

"Well, it's full of birds. I love watching them flying around and seeing all of their antics."

I continued to watch the tree as a bird flew out from beneath a low-hanging branch. "I see some of them."

She pulled out a notebook and was suddenly all business. "Let's get started now. I'll go over everything I can with you, but you'll need to talk to the retirement home administrator when we're done."

I raised an eyebrow, but obeyed her order, taking the seat across from her.

"They can't afford to pay you much, but it's a little." She named a figure. "Is that all right?"

I put my hand on hers. "Tell them not to worry about it. Beth gave me time off to do it. I'm happy to do it for free."

Her smile wobbled. "You have no idea how much this means to all of us."

"I'm happy to help. When you asked me before, I felt bad to not be able to take on the job, but after a cancellation at work, my schedule is much clearer."

"Thank you." She reached into her pocket and pulled

out a tube of cherry LifeSavers, just like the ones she'd offered to the boys. "Would you like one?"

"Uh, no thank you." I hadn't had one since I was a kid, but I remembered them being very sweet.

She shrugged and put them away. "Now, these are the plans that Mila had in place for this year. They shouldn't be too difficult to follow. The party is pretty basic, but it's still special to us. All of the families are invited and my daughter comes up every year from Oregon to attend the party and then bring me back down to Portland for Christmas." Her lips wavered. "It's been a while since she was here last."

"I'm sure she misses you." I didn't know what to say. Neither set of my grandparents had lived in a retirement home before they died, so I wasn't sure how often most people visited their family members. Come to think of it, I hadn't seen too many visitors at the home while I was there, but maybe that was because it was usually during the middle of the day when people had to work.

She went over the plans with me and I took notes on my own notepad to review later. As she'd said, most of it seemed pretty simple.

When we wrapped up the planning session, I looked up at her and said, "When Desi and I were here last time, you were about to tell us about something bad that you thought was going on here—but then you stopped. Are you able to tell me more about that?"

A fearful expression came over her face and her eyes darted back and forth, as if searching the room. "Let's take a walk outside in the gardens."

Wow. She must have been frightened by someone or something if she didn't want to discuss it where we were sitting. No one was close enough to hear us talking, but she obviously wanted even more privacy for what she was about to tell me.

"Sure. Lead the way."

Delilah led me out the door to the concrete patio and then took us on the path to the beautiful gardens I'd noticed when I had followed the boys around the back of the building and found the body.

"Aren't you cold?" While I was wearing my winter coat, she'd come from the toasty warmth of the Great Room and wore nothing but a light sweater over a pink cotton blouse. However, she didn't appear to be affected by the weather.

"No. The cold has never bothered me." She nimbly ducked her walker through a gap in the tall, maze-like hedges and took us off-roading toward the edge of the property.

Now I had my answer about the cliffs. The edges of the bluff were guarded by a railing made of thin logs. It would keep any adult from accidentally falling off the edge, but would do nothing to keep a small inquisitive child from climbing through it.

Below us, the dark blue waters of Puget Sound swirled against the edges of the bluff, only a thin patch of raised land keeping it from eroding the sides. In most of Ericksville, the raised train tracks usually kept storm waters from reaching the bottom of the bluff, but here, the tracks veered inland as they went through Everton. Nothing, however, could keep small sections of dirt from crumbling off of the edge. To our left was a vast, heavily wooded gulch that led down to the beach—typical of the Ericksville area.

"Sometimes when I'm out here, I can imagine that things are the same as they were when I was a child, before everything was so developed. But I guess you can't stop progress." She peered at me, then sat down on a concrete bench that had long been forgotten by the groundskeepers. "Harry Pearson was murdered."

"What? Are you sure?" My heart pounded in my chest. If she was right, something was very wrong at the retirement home.

"When he arrived a couple of months ago, he was healthy as a horse. He once told me that he'd been tired of living at home, so he moved here where he could be around other people. It wasn't until this last week that his health went downhill and his mental state declined. Just like the other two men who died." She looked at me defiantly. "I'm telling you, he was murdered for his money."

"That's a big accusation." I thought for a moment. "Why would you say he was murdered for his money? Did that happen to the other two men?"

"Before they died, both Lenny and Albert blabbed about how they were going to triple their net worth. I'm sure it was some get-rich-quick scheme and that someone conned them into it."

"Did their families say anything about money being missing?" I wasn't sure about her theory, but I wanted to hear more.

"Neither of them had much family to speak of. I'm sure their estates are still tied up in probate." The wind blew her streamers every which way and she ran her fingers through the strands to untangle them.

"Ok," I said slowly. "But what about Harry Pearson? Surely his son would have said something if money was missing."

"I don't know. I haven't heard anything about any missing money, but his death was just like the other two. There has to be a connection."

"I'm not saying I don't believe you, but you're telling me

there is a serial murderer on the loose at the Ericksville Retirement home."

She nodded. "Yes."

I drew in a deep breath. "So you think that someone is drugging elderly men in the home so that they act senile and then convincing them to sign over their money. And then that person murders them somehow and makes it look like they died of natural causes?"

"Yes," she said again. "I know it sounds crazy, but it's too much of a coincidence. I'm not the only one who thinks so."

I thought about it. She was right. The police should at least look into it to determine if there was some sort of connection between their deaths.

"I agree that it does seem suspicious. Have you talked to the police about this?"

"We told Mila about it and she said she'd look into it and contact the police." She gasped and placed her hand over her heart. "Do you think Mila was killed because we told her about this?"

Probably she was, but I wasn't going to tell that to Delilah. "I'm sure you had nothing to do with her death." That was the truth at least. I was 100 percent certain that Delilah hadn't been directly responsible for Mila's death.

She looked out at the water. "I hope you're right."

The temperature had dropped while we were outside and the sky had turned gray. Miniscule snowflakes fell from the sky, peppering us with icy coldness.

"We'd better get back inside." I didn't want to be responsible for Delilah slipping and falling on the wet ground, especially when we were so far away from the home.

"All right," she said as she rose from the bench. I think our conversation had tired her out, because it took her twice as long to get back to the home as it had to get out to the gardens. When I had her safely ensconced in her favorite chair in the Great Room, I whispered in her ear, "I'll make sure the police investigate, ok? I promise."

She gave me a curt nod to show she'd heard.

"I need to take care of some of the party planning, but if you're still out here when I'm done, I'll come by."

She grabbed my hand. "Thank you, Jill." She released my hand and stared out the window at her beloved birds.

I reluctantly left her alone and went out to the lobby.

The receptionist was at her station behind the desk, so I asked her if she could point me in the direction of the administrator.

"Alfie?" She pointed at the hallway behind her. "His office is right down this hall, but he's not in right now."

"Oh, ok. Do you know when he'll be back? I need to talk with him about the retirement home's Christmas party." I smiled at her. "I've recently taken over the party planning."

"I'm glad someone is going to do the party. I've heard the residents really enjoy it." She shrugged. "But I have no clue when Alfred is coming back. He's been gone for a while to the hospital."

I heard the word hospital and immediately wondered if there was another possible victim who'd suddenly fallen ill.

"Oh, I hope everything is ok." I smiled sweetly at her.

Before she could respond, the nurse I'd seen earlier came out of the door at the far end of the hallway. She twisted her ring around her finger as she walked past, but didn't make eye contact with me.

The receptionist looked at her, then leaned closer to me so the nurse wouldn't hear. "He's never around because his thirteen-year-old daughter is in the hospital. She's on the list for a kidney transplant, but I don't know how much longer she can hold on."

The thought of a kid being so sick socked me in the gut. It seemed like every day I was hearing more and more bad news. "Oh, that's rough. I don't blame him for missing work. I'll stop by another day, ok? It's not really urgent."

She gave me a thumbs-up sign. "Sounds good."

I said goodbye and left the retirement home, feeling a sense of relief when I walked out the front doors. The historic building was beautiful, but it had started to feel oppressive.

I called Desi before I went in to work and asked her to find out from Tomàs if the police were investigating the deaths of the three men at the retirement home. She promised she'd call him and let me know what he said.

12

*L*ate that afternoon, I took some time off to join Desi at one of the weekly MUMs group stroller walks. I figured that even though it was time spent away from work, I'd be a better worker if I got some exercise and fresh air. Plus, I wanted to find out if she'd heard anything from Tomàs about the mens' deaths.

When I arrived at Lighthouse Park with Ella, Desi was stretching lightly, using Lina's stroller for balance. Behind her, other moms in our walking group milled around. It was so cold that I could see my breath puffing out in front of me like little clouds as I pushed my stroller toward her. Even this late in the day, the grass still had frost on it, or maybe it was some snow leftover from the flakes that had fallen briefly that morning. Whatever the case, it was freezing cold and I was having a hard time convincing myself to stay at the park instead of going somewhere for a hot cup of coffee.

Before I could open my mouth to speak, she said, "No, Tomàs hasn't called me back yet about the investigation. I don't even know if he will." She handed me a cup of coffee from her café. "Here."

I reached for it and wrapped my hands around the cup for warmth. "How did you know?"

She sighed. "You always want coffee. I figured bringing you hot coffee on a cold afternoon was a safe bet."

I smiled at her. "Well, thanks." I sipped the coffee until the contents were low enough in the cup that they wouldn't slosh through the opening when I went over bumps.

"So where are we going today?" I looked around. The ranks had swelled and there were now about a dozen moms with their babies waiting in the park.

"Not sure. Lisa hasn't said yet." Desi pointed to our illustrious leader, who was dressed in tight running pants and a long sleeved workout shirt, perfectly matched of course.

"I love this time of year." I clutched the warm coffee cup between my hands and gazed at the Christmas tree in Lighthouse Park. Every year, the town decorated the tall tree with colorful lights and a bright star at the top. Although it wasn't dark yet, the tree was lit and sparkled against the white backdrop of the lighthouse.

Lisa signaled to us that it was time to go and moved her stroller onto the sidewalk. We all trotted along behind her. About twenty minutes into the walk, Desi's phone rang.

She pulled it out. "It's Tomàs," she said with surprise. "I really didn't think I'd hear anything from him until he got home from work tonight."

"Answer it!" I hissed. I glanced at Lisa. She wouldn't be happy to see one of us on the phone, but if Tomàs had information about the suspicious deaths, I wanted to know ASAP.

She glanced at Lisa too, then surreptitiously lifted the phone to her ear while still keeping pace with the rest of the group. "Uh huh ... uh huh."

I stopped, causing her to run into me and set off a chain

reaction of collisions with the other moms and strollers behind us. Lisa turned to glare at me.

"Sorry!" I called out.

She eyed me, then turned around and continued on.

By this time, Desi had finished her phone conversation.

"So?"

"So, all of the men besides Pearson were terminally ill. The police aren't investigating because there's nothing suspicious about it."

"But Delilah said they were in good health."

"Maybe they were, but when you're terminally ill, you can go downhill fast." Desi changed her grip on the stroller as Lisa took us up one of the streets that climbed away from the ferry dock.

"I guess. But how do you explain them talking about getting rich from something and then the rapid decline in their mental faculties?"

She shrugged. "I don't know. Tomàs said he'd make sure someone dug deeper into it, but right now, they don't think it had anything to do with Mila's death."

"Which leaves them suspecting Will."

"Yep." She stared down at Lina and idly rearranged the blanket she'd wrapped around her daughter.

"But what if there is something weird about their deaths?"

"Are you still on this?" She turned around to briefly lock eyes with me. "You really believe Delilah, don't you?"

"I do. She doesn't seem like the kind of person that would just come up with random conspiracy theories." Desi brushed a wisp of hair back from her face.

"Ok, well, if she's right, then why did Pearson's death break the pattern? And why hasn't his family said anything about him having money conned out of him? I'm pretty sure they'd have raised a fuss if it were true."

"I don't have an answer for that." We'd returned to the park and Lisa was having us do some cooldown stretching. Although it hadn't seemed like much of a workout while we were pushing the strollers, I could feel it now in my warm muscles and tired legs.

"Do you think Tomàs is really going to make sure they investigate further? I promised Delilah that I'd make sure the police took her claims seriously." I pulled my foot up toward my back to stretch my quadriceps.

Desi sighed. "I'll do my best to make him understand, but I can't make any guarantees."

"Thanks, Desi."

"Honestly, Jill?" she said. "I think we need to find out what happened to those men. That's got to be the whole key to this thing. I can't keep the news about Will being a suspect from my mom much longer, so we've got to help move things along."

"I agree. I'll ask around tomorrow at Ericksville Heights when I go talk to the administrator there about the party. Maybe someone else knows something."

"Let me know if you find anything out. See you." She turned her stroller around and headed in the direction of her house.

I continued home, my calves burning as I hiked up the hill to our house. Some of the neighbors had decorated their houses, but the house below us that had belonged to Samuel Westen was conspicuously dark. I wondered what Anna Westen planned to do with her father's house and if we'd have a new next door neighbor anytime soon. It was so cold that my chest hurt with every breath of frigid air, but it was all worth it when I walked into our warm house and Ella and I flopped down on the couch to rest.

"Tough day, honey?" Adam said from the kitchen where he was making dinner.

"Something like that." I didn't want to tell him that I was worn out from a stroller walk, although I was also mentally exhausted by my conversation with Delilah earlier in the day. I'd made a promise to her, and if the police weren't going to take it seriously, I'd have to do some investigating on my own until I had enough evidence to get them interested.

13

I didn't have any client appointments the next morning, so I decided to visit the retirement home to see if the administrator, Alfred Dolan, was in.

"Hi." I flashed a smile at the receptionist, Dana, who knew me by now.

"Hello."

"Is Alfred Dolan in today?"

She nodded. "He is, but he's busy at the moment." She leaned in and whispered, "There's a police detective and Mr. Pearson's son in there with him."

"Ok, no problem. I'll wait for him. Can you let me know when he's free?"

"Sure." She motioned to a seat in the hallway near the administrative staff's offices. "You can have a seat there if you'd like."

"Thanks." I sat down in the chair nearest to the closed door on the end that bore a plaque with Alfred's name on it.

The doors themselves must have been paper thin, because I could hear almost everything they were saying inside. The detective appeared to be interviewing Chas

Pearson about his father's finances, which he seemed to object to because his voice rose higher in volume as the meeting wore on. I needed to remember to tell Delilah that the police must be taking her theories into consideration if they were talking to Chas.

"No. How many times do I have to tell you that my father did not fall victim to some scam. He died naturally, in his sleep. I don't understand why you insist on putting us through this."

The detective responded, "There have been some inconsistencies brought to light and we need to make sure that no stone is left unturned in our investigation."

"Well," Chas huffed, "you're going to be hearing from my lawyers."

The door opened and I flattened myself against the back of my chair and pretended to be engrossed in something on my phone.

Chas stormed out, followed by the police detective, who wore his badge on a chain around his neck.

"Thank you for your assistance," the detective said to a man who I presumed was Alfred Dolan.

"Of course. I was happy to help." Alfred shuddered. "I hate the thought that something untoward was happening here at the retirement home. I'm so glad that we got this matter cleared up."

The policeman nodded. "We are too. For now, this matter is closed, but if you think of anything we should know, here's my business card." He handed Alfred a small white card.

Alfred took it and put the card in his pants pocket, then stood there watching as the policeman walked away. I wasn't entirely sure if he'd seen me sitting right there in front of him or not because he hadn't yet greeted me.

I put my phone back in my purse and stood. "Mr. Dolan?"

He didn't answer for a moment, then seemed to collect himself and focused his attention on me. "Yes, I'm Alfred Dolan. How may I help you?"

I held out my hand. "I'm Jill Andrews. Delilah talked to you about having me coordinate the Christmas party? I was hoping you might have time to chat with me for a bit about the event."

He looked confused for a second. "Oh, right. You were here a few days ago, weren't you? When the preschool class was here."

"I was."

"I thought I recognized you." He glanced at his watch. "I was just about to head out to grab a bite to eat. Do you think we could meet in an hour?"

"Uh, sure." I'd have to stick around the retirement home because there wouldn't be enough time to get anything done back at the Boathouse, but I didn't mind having the extra time to visit Delilah. "I can meet you here in an hour."

"Great." He ran his fingers through his hair and gave a deep sigh. He must have caught the odd look I gave him, because he said, "Sorry. It's already been a long day."

"I saw the detective and Chas Pearson were here. Chas didn't seem too happy."

"No. He wasn't. And I don't blame him. His father was a sick, elderly man. It wasn't terribly surprising when he passed. But for some reason the police think there was something suspicious about it." He shook his head. "Our recreation director died recently and everyone's pretty shaken up about it, I think."

I gave him a sympathetic look. "I'm sorry for your loss. I was here when they found her body."

"You were?" He examined me more closely. "Oh, that was the day the preschool visited, wasn't it?" He started walking toward the lobby. "Anyway, I need to step out. I'll see you in an hour."

Before he was able to leave the building, one of the residents, a woman with fluffy white hair and red lipstick, stopped him. I paused, stuck behind him and her.

"Alfred," she said, "can I come and talk to you later today? I need to move some money from my retirement investment funds into my checking account and I can't seem to figure out the online transfer form." She sighed and her eyes were troubled. "I don't know why they make it so difficult."

He put his hand on her upper arm reassuringly. "I'll put it on my schedule for this afternoon. Don't worry, Mabel—we'll figure it out."

"Thanks, Alfred." A look of relief came over her and she looked at him adoringly. "You're always so helpful."

Alfred may have been a bit scattered, but at least the residents seemed to like him. I made my way into the Great Room, thinking about Alfred and Chas. I didn't see Delilah in there, but I did see someone familiar—Anna Westen. She was talking to one of the residents and explaining something on a clipboard, so I walked near her and gave her a small wave, but didn't say anything. She smiled back at me and held up a finger.

I settled into a chair nearby and waited for her. I hadn't seen her often since her father was murdered last spring, and I made a mental note to catch up with her over coffee sometime soon.

"Jill." She came up and hugged me. "This is a nice surprise. What are you doing here?" She looked around. "Are you visiting someone?"

I laughed. "Not today. The retirement home lost their recreation director recently and they needed someone to complete the plans for their annual Christmas party."

Her lips turned down. "I heard about Mila's death. She was always so nice and polite when I'd come here to visit clients."

"That's what I've heard about her too. It's scary that they don't know who killed her." I glanced involuntarily at the backyard.

"No kidding. When I've visited clients here over the last few days to have them sign their estate planning documents, they're all a little concerned by her murder. And rightfully so."

I sat back in my chair and regarded her. Anna worked for an estate planning attorney as a paralegal. It was still bothering me that Chas Pearson was denying any financial problems with his father's affairs. Was he lying or telling the truth?

"Can I ask you something I'd been wondering about?" I asked.

"Sure, what's on your mind?" Anna gazed at me with curiosity.

"If one of the residents here was a victim of a con prior to their death, why would their family deny that it happened?"

"Well, there are a couple of reasons. For one, if it wasn't much money, the family might not want to embarrass their loved one by admitting they were conned. Secondly, I would think that if the police got word of such a thing happening, they'd want to launch an investigation. That could delay disbursement of any inheritance while the police investigate." She scrutinized me. "Why, did that happen here?"

I stared down at the table in front of me and then met her eyes. "I don't know. Maybe."

"If it did, you need to tell someone. Elder abuse is a big problem in retirement homes because the residents are often very vulnerable." She set the papers she was carrying on the table and sat down across from me. "If it happened here, you should tell the retirement home administrator or the police."

I didn't want to push the subject because I wasn't sure what had happened and was only working off of theories. "The police have been notified that it's a possibility, but I was just curious what would happen."

She checked her watch and stood, gathering up her papers again. "I'm not sure what would happen to the family member perpetrating the cover-up, but I don't know how someone could do that to an elderly relative. I disliked my father and I still wouldn't have done anything to keep the police from investigating any wrongdoings against him."

"I agree." My mind was jumbled with thoughts of evil relatives.

A thought occurred to me. Anna said she had been to Ericksville Heights many times. What if one of the deceased men was a client of hers? There may not have been any relatives to ask about their finances, but Anna would have their bank account information if her law firm was tasked with administering the estate.

"Anna?" I asked.

She looked up sharply. "Did you think of something else?"

I pressed my lips together, then spoke. "I know you're not able to divulge if one of the deceased men, Albert Wendil or Lenny Landers, were clients of yours, but if they were, perhaps you could check their bank records to see if there are any suspicious transactions."

She eyed me and said carefully, "If one of them was a client, it's possible that I could do that. I'll call you later to talk about it, ok?"

"Thank you. That would be great." I smiled at her. "Hey, I haven't seen you around your father's house in a while. Do you have plans to sell it?"

She frowned. "I'm not sure yet what to do about it. I hate the idea of selling the house since it belonged to my mother's family, but it's such a big expense to maintain. I may rent it out or something—maybe have it as a vacation rental."

I nodded. She'd mentioned the possibility to me not long after her father's death. I wasn't keen on having the house below ours as a vacation rental because there would probably be loud parties and increased traffic on our hill, but I understood what Anna meant. An old house like Westen's couldn't be cheap to keep up. Besides, maybe having it as a vacation rental wouldn't be as bad as I'd thought. And it would definitely be better than having the property subdivided for a dozen more houses, as her father had planned.

We chatted about the house for a while, then said our goodbyes and Anna left to return to work. I walked over to the lobby and Alfred's office to see if he'd come back yet. An hour had passed and his door was open, so I knocked on it.

14

*A*lfred's head bobbed up, as if he were startled. "Oh. I'd forgotten. Come in." He beckoned for me to come and sit in front of his desk.

How could someone forget an appointment in the space of an hour? I entered the room and took the seat opposite him. Mila's name was on the door as well and I assumed that the organized desk in the corner was hers. File cabinets lined one wall and an abstract art painting had been hung on the wall next to it.

I looked longingly at Mila's desk for a split second before sitting down across from Alfred. While I assumed that the police had gone through Mila's desk, there was always the possibility that they'd missed something, especially if it was in regard to the deaths they'd deemed unsuspicious. What were the chances that I could get some time alone in here though? Alfred had just returned from somewhere, so he was probably settling in for a while.

He folded his hands on the desk. "What can I help you with?"

I took out my notebook. "I wanted to confirm that it's ok

for me to instruct the staff on how to arrange the tables and for the kitchen to provide food for the event."

He smiled. "Of course. We're so happy that you're taking this on. Our residents were quite saddened by the news that the party was cancelled."

"I have a few other small things too." I went over them with him and he helped me figure out a few logistics for the party. He had a box full of photos of previous Christmas parties that I thought would make a nice display. I'd only been in there for twenty minutes when he popped up from his chair and grabbed his jacket.

"I've got to run. I have a... uh... doctor's appointment to go to."

For him, or for his daughter? Having a child that was so sick must have been difficult and I wanted to say something, but since he hadn't told me himself about his daughter's illness, I didn't want to ask about her.

"It's great that you're able to have such a flexible schedule here. It seems like with so many jobs nowadays, they don't want to understand that people have families." I motioned to the picture of a young girl on his desk. "Is that your daughter?"

He gazed at it and his anxious demeanor softened for a moment. "Yes. She's thirteen." He looked up at me and uttered a harsh laugh. "This job may allow for some flexibility in my schedule, but our insurance isn't worth anything."

"That's too bad." I pressed my lips together. "Health care costs are insane."

He glanced at the photo again. "Especially if you have a major illness." He gestured to the other desk in the room and then to the box of old photos. "You can sit at Mila's desk to work on this if you'd like. I usually keep this door locked and only Mila and I had the key, but I think it will be ok if you use it for today. Just make sure to lock up when you're done."

I glanced at the other desk, which was neat and tidy, a stark contrast to his messy workspace. I couldn't help but wonder what the desk contained. If Mila had been killed because she'd been looking into the suspicious deaths of two of the residents, maybe there would be some sort of clue in there.

"Sure. That would be great."

He scurried out of there, leaving me all alone in a room that was full of possible clues. I peeked my head out the door, but he was long gone. I didn't want to alert anyone that I was snooping, so I closed the door partway.

Now, where to start? I scanned the room. The file cabinet or Mila's desk were the best bets for information. I figured the file cabinet would be more difficult to get access to if Alfred came back, so I started there.

First, I pulled out the medical records for the two men that had died first. Exactly like Desi said, their medical records showed that they both had less than a year to live due to terminal illnesses. I felt a pang of guilt as I reviewed their medical history without their permission, but they were both dead and I was trying to right a possible wrong.

Then, I plucked Harry Pearson's file out of the cabinet and spread it out atop the open drawer. There was nothing in there about him having any sort of terminal illness. Like Delilah had said, up until about a week before his death, he was perfectly healthy for an eighty-eight-year-old man. I'd seen him with my own eyes a few weeks ago, in robust health as he helped plan his company's Christmas party. It was certainly possible that he'd died of natural causes, but if his mental decline had occurred just like the others, there was also a chance that the deaths were related.

I heard footsteps in the hallway, shoved the file back in the drawer and closed it as quietly as possible, then slid onto the chair behind Mila's desk.

The nurse I'd seen earlier came in, wearing a nametag that read *Nurse Fluge*. I smiled at her and said, "Good morning." My heart was pounding. That had been too close.

She eyed me. "What are you doing in here? You shouldn't be back here."

"Alfred said I could use Mila's desk while I'm here working on the Christmas party."

She huffed. "I don't know why he'd say that. Nobody is allowed back here except staff."

I didn't know whether to leave or stay. But Alfred had told me that I could stay and I hadn't managed to get much snooping in before Nurse Fluge had arrived.

"I suppose I'm a member of the staff—at least until after the Christmas party."

She glared at me, but just gestured to the file cabinet. "I need some patient files."

"Of course." I made a show of rearranging some papers I'd left on Mila's desk.

Out of the corner of my eye, I saw her move over to the drawers containing the medical records and heard the sounds of files being pulled out of the thick outer files folders, then the drawer slamming shut.

"Don't forget to lock the door behind you when you leave." She strode out the room, her rubber-bottomed shoes smacking against the vinyl floors.

When I couldn't hear her footsteps any more, I let out the breath I'd been holding. The file cabinet closest to Alfred's desk had been labeled "Employee Records" and I wanted to check those out before Nurse Fluge returned again.

I quickly went through the staff records but didn't find anything amiss. Then, I went back to Mila's desk and sorted through her drawers. There was an article from the newspaper about elder abuse that she'd printed out, but that wasn't necessarily a smoking gun since she did work at a retirement home. I finished the work that I needed to do for the party and stood to leave.

A book on the corner of Mila's desk caught my eye. It was the newest romance novel from one of my favorite authors and I'd been meaning to grab a copy of it. The corners of the pages were pristine and the spine uncracked. I doubted she'd had a chance to read it before her death. I picked it up to read the back cover and a piece of paper floated out of the book and onto the desk.

The scrap of notebook paper contained only two words printed on it in blue ink—*Calvado Bldg.*

I'd never heard of the building, but there must have been some reason Mila had stuck the note in the book. If she hadn't read it yet, it was unlikely that she'd used it as a bookmark, so why was it there?

Well, Calvado Building should be something I could look up easily. I reached into my purse for my cell phone. It wasn't in the side pocket where I usually kept it. I rummaged around in my giant purse for a few minutes, but couldn't find it, so I started unloading the contents on to the desk in front of me. Ella's diapers and wipes, my wallet, my keys, a bottle of hand sanitizer, a plastic baggie full of Cheerios, a random assortment of crayons and other small toys, but no phone. Shoot. I was sure I'd had it with me when I left the house that morning, so I must have left it in the car.

I didn't think anyone would miss the scrap of paper, so I

tossed it into my purse to check on it later. It might not mean anything, but I had so little to go on that I didn't want to discount a possible clue.

I checked to see if Delilah was in the Great Room, but she still wasn't there. I hoped she was feeling ok, but I didn't know her very well, and I didn't want to bother her in her room if she was sleeping, so I left for work at the Boathouse.

15

I took a late lunch break and met Desi for lunch at the teriyaki place down the street from the Boathouse.

"This is delicious," she said as she bit into a piece of grilled chicken teriyaki. "Don't tell any of my customers, but the soups and sandwiches we serve at the BeansTalk start to bore me after a while. There's only so many bowls of minestrone I can eat before I want to heave it against a wall."

I poured teriyaki sauce on my food, forming a pool of the sticky, sweet sauce on top of the mounded rice and strips of chicken. "I don't know how you can work there every day and not be five hundred pounds. I'd eat all of the leftover pastries at the end of the day."

"Someone who works for the food bank comes and picks up any perishable leftovers. The food bank gets some fresh pastries to give out and a happy side effect is that I'm not tempted by leftovers." She shoveled a forkful of rice into her mouth.

"Has Tomàs said anything further about the investigation into the deaths at the retirement home?" I asked.

"He said there isn't one." She shrugged. "Pearson's son said there's no money missing from his father's accounts and without any family members filing complaints, the police have no reason to investigate it further."

"So that's it? This is going to be upsetting for Delilah. She's convinced herself that there is something sinister going on."

"I know." Desi's face fell and she set down her fork. "But maybe there isn't. Wouldn't that be better?"

"But what if there is?" I peered at her. "What if Chas Pearson is lying about his father's accounts?"

She gave me a skeptical look. "Why would he do that?"

"I told you how fast he cancelled the company Christmas party after his father's death and he shut down the business without any warning to his employees." I locked eyes with her. "What if he wanted control of his father's finances immediately and didn't want there to be an investigation?"

"So he killed his own father?"

"I don't know. At the very least, he may have covered up his murder." I sighed. "Or maybe it's nothing."

"But Mila's death wasn't nothing. Let's think about this. The news hasn't reported anything about possible motives into her death and everyone at the retirement home loved her. Why would someone kill her?"

"I don't know." I pushed some grains of rice around my plate with the tines of the fork, forming a neat pile on the side. I wished all of life could be that simple. "Let's say there is something going on there. I think Chas is a jerk, but if it wasn't him who killed those men and Mila, who was it?"

"The money is always a motive. If those men were conned, where did the money go? And how did whoever killed them know they had money to take in the first place?"

"Well, Pearson obviously had money because he owned a successful company in the area. That one is easy. But the others? Hmm ..." I wished I'd gone through the last file cabinet in Alfred's office to see what was in the resident's files. "The other men were terminally ill, just as Tomàs told you. There was something though. Mila had an article in her desk about scams people ran on the elderly. Convincing them to transfer money into another investment account and then stealing the money is pretty common. But it would have to be someone the men trusted."

"So who would she have told about her suspicions?"

"Alfred Dolan, the administrator. Maybe Nurse Fluge in regard to their health. The receptionist, Dana, had access to all of the records too. I suppose there could have been someone else at the home that I don't know of."

"That's a lot of suspects." Desi frowned. "No wonder the police seem stuck on Will—he's the easiest one to target first."

"Remember Anna Westen?"

"Yeah." Her head shot up. "How is she involved in all of this?"

"Well, she's not really, but since she's a paralegal for an estate planning law firm, she meets with clients often at Ericksville Heights." I fiddled with my water glass. "I may have suggested to her that if one of the deceased men was a client of hers that she should check their bank records for suspicious transactions."

Desi's eyes lit up. "If she can find anything, that could blow open the whole investigation. The money trail should lead to whoever conned those men and probably killed them."

"Right—and to whomever Mila confided in by error. But we don't even know if Anna can get that information."

"So what else can we do in the meantime?" Desi asked. "Let's try this from another angle. Did you find anything out about the other suspects we talked about? That nurse, or the administrator? Or even the receptionist?"

"I did a little snooping but there weren't any major red flags. The administrator, Alfred, is well respected by the residents, but he has a daughter who's undergoing expensive medical treatments. He could use the money." I paused, remembering how the elderly woman had asked Albert for help with transferring money between bank accounts. Had other residents asked him for help as well? If so, he'd know a great deal about their finances. I continued, "Nurse Fluge has access to the patient files in Albert's office, so both of them could have known about the diagnosis of terminal illnesses for the first two victims. If those men died all of a sudden, no one would have said anything and their tracks would have been covered. By the same token, Dana had access too, whenever Alfred wasn't in the office. I don't know how any of them would have known how much money the victims had or how Pearson fits in with it all."

"Maybe you could ask Delilah next time you go there if she has any thoughts about how they'd know about a resident's finances."

"I don't know if that's a good idea. I'm worried that she'll do some snooping of her own and I want to keep her out of this as much as possible for her safety."

"Sheesh, I didn't even think about that. But you need to take some of your own advice. Don't make waves because we don't know who the real killer is."

"I know," I said grimly.

16

The next morning, I stopped in at the retirement home to talk to the kitchen staff about the party. When I was done, I checked for Delilah again. I hadn't realized how worried I'd been about her until I saw the familiar silver streamers at the front of the Great Room near the window.

Her face lit up when she saw me. "Hi, Jill. I'm so happy to see you. Have a seat." She motioned to the seat on the other side of the table. I sat down and put my notebook on the table in front of me and my purse on the ground.

"I'm glad to see you too. I checked for you yesterday a couple of times while I was here, but you must have been in your room." I looked at her more closely. Her complexion was wan, although she'd tried to hide it with rouge and pink lipstick. "Are you feeling ok?"

"Oh, sure." She waved her hand in the air dismissively. "Good as ever. When you get to be my age, you have your good days and bad days. I was feeling slightly under the weather yesterday, and I had my meals brought in so I could rest."

I scrutinized her expression. I hoped she was telling me the truth as I'd become quite fond of her. "Well, if you start feeling poorly, please tell the nurse."

"Nurse Fluge?" She looked around. "She's only been here for the past month and she's really odd. Always has a sour expression on her face."

I laughed. "I've noticed. But seriously. Take care of yourself."

"I will. Thank you for worrying about me." She lowered her voice and asked, "Did you find anything out about the matter we discussed?"

"Yes," I whispered back. "The police are looking into it. I saw them with Chas Pearson yesterday morning. He seemed upset by their questions and implications. Claimed there was nothing amiss with his father's finances."

She sat back. "Hmm. Well, let me know if you hear anything else."

"I will." She didn't look well and I didn't want to tell her that the police appeared to be dropping the investigation after speaking with Chas. "Do you know how the person who conned those men out of their money knew that they were well-off?"

"If it were me, I'd look in our application forms."

"Application forms?" They had to apply to live at Ericksville Heights?

"Yes. Before we're offered a room here, there's paperwork to fill out. One of the things is a list of our savings and investment account balances." She laughed. "This place isn't cheap and they want to make sure we're not going to run out on the bill."

"That makes sense." With everyone who had access to the file cabinets in Alfred's office, anyone could have found out which residents would make good targets.

"You look busy," she said, looking at the laptop sticking out the padded section of my purse.

"I stopped in here before work to talk to the kitchen staff about the party. Everything is going great with the planning."

She grinned. "Wonderful. We could definitely use a pick-me-up around here."

Delilah was right though. I did need to get to work. I'd spent so much time on the retirement home's Christmas party that I was behind on my own work at the Boathouse.

"I'd better go, but I'll see you at the party on Sunday, if not before, ok?"

She nodded. "Have a nice day, dear." She returned to staring out the window at some birds, which were searching for something in the grass next to the patio.

17

I got into my car and drove to the Boathouse, but instead of starting work, I decided to pay Chas Pearson a visit. I had his office's address on file, so I dashed inside and pulled his address from the system. I also printed off a copy of the invoice for what the Pearson Company owed. Beth had told me that we could write off the amount that they owed, but I figured it would be a good reason for me to visit him at work.

Chas's company, Pearson & Associates, was located in a three-story building with large glass windows that spanned each floor from top to bottom. I'd expected to find it in a shared office space, but the company name was the only one on the front door, so it must have been bigger than I'd thought. Then again, I had no clue what exactly Chas's company did.

A receptionist wearing a black headset sat behind a high, horseshoe-shaped desk. I approached the counter and smiled at her. My reward was a blank stare and one finger held in the air to warn me that she was on the phone. I waited a few minutes until she was free from the call.

Finally, she looked up at me. "Yes? What can I do to help you?"

"I'm looking for Chas Pearson."

"Do you have an appointment with him?"

"No, but I just need a minute of his time." I smiled at her.

Her demeanor didn't change. "And what may I tell him this visit is about?"

"I'm Jill Andrews, from the Boathouse Event Center in Ericksville and I need to talk to him about an event that his father had planned."

She dialed a number and spoke into the microphone of her headset. "Mr. Pearson? I have a Jill Andrews at the front desk for you. She'd like to meet about some event your father had planned." She paused while he answered. "I'll tell her." Looking back up at me, she said, "He'll see you, but he only has a few minutes, so make it quick."

"Of course. I'm sure he's a very busy man." I thought back to how angry he'd been about the police wasting his time when I'd seen him at the retirement home.

"Take the elevator to the third floor, last door on the left." She hit a button on her desk and the elevator doors slid open like magic.

I entered the elevator and hit the button for Floor 3. When I stepped out, I entered a small windowless room with a door to each side. I was glad Desi wasn't with me because this would have set off her claustrophobia.

Which way had she told me to go? I'd been too busy thinking about Chas Pearson to hear which way I should go. To the left seemed more promising, so I pushed open the door.

I was rewarded with another hallway, but at least this one had some natural light from skylights high overhead and was lined with doors on one side. I followed the carpeted hallway to the end and knocked on the door marked *Chas Pearson*.

"Come in."

I opened the door slightly and peeked in. Chas sat behind a desk that was perpendicular to the full-length window and he was engrossed in something on his computer.

I entered the room and he spun around his chair to face me. Recognition dawned on his face.

"I've seen you before—at the retirement home, right?" He cocked his head to the side. "I thought Gia said you were from the Boathouse?"

"I am from the Boathouse. Sorry for any confusion. I'm helping the retirement home out with their Christmas party too. I'm not sure if you heard, but their recreation director was killed last week."

He didn't react to my mention of Mila's murder.

"I hadn't heard." He slid his chair forward and leaned on his desk. "Now, what can I do for you?"

I pulled the invoice from my bag and set it on his desk. He picked it up and scanned the document.

"This is for the Pearson Company's Christmas party my father had planned at the Boathouse?"

I looked him in the eyes. "Yes. There's a small outstanding balance."

"And you came all the way over here for this?" He reached into his desk drawer and removed a checkbook.

He had a point. I hadn't completely thought this through. "I wanted to offer my condolences for your father's death in person. Although I mainly dealt with the human resources department, I met with your father a few times about the party. I was sorry to hear of his passing. He was such a nice man."

"Sometimes," he said under his breath as he scribbled on the check. He ripped it out of the checkbook with a flourish and presented it to me.

"It must have been hard for you to return to the retirement home after his death."

He eyed me, then cleared his throat. "I didn't have much of a choice. I was summoned there by the police because they had some ridiculous notion about my father's death. He was a sick old man, nothing more."

I gave him a sympathetic smile. "They're probably trying to cover all of their bases." I stood from the desk and pushed the chair in. "My friend at the retirement home told me that two men who died recently were victims of a scam." I pressed my lips together and shook my head. "Who would do such a thing? I'm glad to hear that your father wasn't affected by it though. I'd hate to think of him being victimized like that. But I heard that they may have identified the person who was conning the residents out of their money."

His face blanched and he ducked his head down to place the checkbook in a bottom drawer. When he sat upright again, his complexion had returned to its normal color. "That's good to hear," he said with a forced smile. "Maybe now the police will leave me alone."

"I hope so." I waved the check in the air. "Thank you for the payment, and let me know if you ever want to have an event at the Boathouse. We have an in-house catering department and can take care of almost any event, big or small."

"I'll keep you in mind." He lowered his eyes to his computer keyboard and tapped at it.

I'd been dismissed. I returned to the lobby, passing by the receptionist, who barely looked at me.

"Bye," I said cheerfully. In return, I received a tight-lipped smile.

On the way back to the Boathouse, I mulled Chas's reaction to my statement about the police being close to catching the con artist. He may have claimed to the police that his father hadn't been victimized, but his expression in his office had told a different story.

So, now I had indirect confirmation that Harry Pearson had been a victim of the same con as the other two men, but I wasn't sure where that left me. Had Chas orchestrated the whole thing, or was he just covering up so there wouldn't be an investigation into his father's death? He didn't seem to have a close relationship with his father, so I wouldn't have been surprised to hear that he'd killed him. Whatever the case, my earlier impression of him hadn't changed—he wasn't a nice man.

When I got back to my office, I realized that I'd forgotten my notebook on the table Delilah had been sitting at. I thought about leaving it there and picking it up the next day, but I needed to finalize some of the plans for the retirement home Christmas party and I wasn't confident that I'd remember everything I needed to do that afternoon.

The parking lot wasn't as full as it had been when I'd come that morning and I easily found a spot closer to the home. I half jogged, half walked up to the building, then slowed as I entered the lobby.

"Back so soon, Jill?" Dana asked. "I swear you're here all the time."

"I'm starting to feel like that." I stopped to catch my breath. "I forgot something in the Great Room."

"Oh, ok. I hope you find it." A resident had walked up to the desk and she turned her face up to listen to what they were saying.

Delilah was still in the same place when I returned to the Great Room.

"I thought you'd be back." She handed me the notebook.

I leaned in and whispered into her ear. "You were right about Harry Pearson. I talked to his son today, and even though he claims his father was never a victim of the con artist, I'm sure he was lying."

Her eyes danced. "I knew it."

"I'm still not sure how it all fits together, but I'm working on it, ok?"

"I'll ask around and see if any of the residents have thought of anything else that might give us a lead in the investigation."

I noticed she said "us." I narrowed my eyes at her. "You aren't doing anything dangerous, are you?"

She gave me a "who, me?" look. "Of course not. But it doesn't hurt to make some discreet inquiries."

In a low voice, I said, "Ok, but please don't do anything to put yourself in danger. Remember, Mila was killed because of it."

"I remember," she said grimly.

I said goodbye to her and hurried out to my car. When I unlocked the door, I realized that something had been left on the windshield of my car. It looked like maybe someone had lost a small toy doll and put it on my car for its owner to find. I picked it up to move it to a more secure location and noticed that it wasn't an ordinary doll.

The doll's face wore a bright smile, but someone had

wrapped a miniature set of lights around her neck. A small piece of paper flew out of her dress and fluttered to the ground. I stared at it for a few seconds and then rescued it before it could fly away. I wasn't sure I wanted to read the writing on it, but I forced myself to do so.

Stay out of this.

18

———

$\mathcal{I}$ wasn't looking forward to dinner at my in-laws the next day, especially considering how the last dinner had gone. Tania had left in a huff and disappeared for a few days and Will had gone out afterwards, met up with an old girlfriend, and become a murder suspect. With any luck, this dinner would go better.

Judging by the way that Tania and Will were glaring at each other across the table, this wasn't going much better. At least they were both still in the same room.

"Can you please put some Brussels sprouts on my plate?" Desi asked, holding out her plate to her mother. The table was so crowded that passing the large bowls and platters of food was difficult.

"Sure, honey." Beth gave her a scoopful, then turned to Tania and held up the serving spoon. "Would you like some? I bet the girls would be more likely to eat them if their mother did. They should eat more vegetables." She nodded at their veggie-less plates.

Tania gave her a look of disdain. "They eat plenty of vegetables, as do I. We just don't like Brussels sprouts."

Beth stared at her for a moment, then set the spoon back in the bowl and stood from the table. "I'm going to see if there are any more rolls left." She grabbed the empty wicker basket from the table.

"Uh, I'd better help her," Lincoln said.

Desi and I exchanged glances. Tomàs was fortunate that he'd had to work tonight. Beth had been making subtle digs at Tania all evening. So far, Tania had deflected them, but I wasn't sure how much longer that would last.

"So, Bella, how are you liking school this year?" Desi asked.

"It's fine." Will's oldest daughter drew circles on her plate with the tip of her fork.

"Bella is a wonderful artist," Tania interjected. "She's been taking lessons after school in painting with watercolors."

Adam smiled at Bella. "That's wonderful. Your dad was always into art when he was a kid. I remember him slaving over a pencil sketch for hours in high school."

She glanced up at him, then looked at her mom. "Can I be excused, please?"

Tania met her eyes. "Sure. Go ahead, honey."

"Can I too?" Maya asked.

"And me?" Claire said.

"Finish your salmon and then you can go play," Will said.

They shoveled the food into their mouths and then jumped up from the table and ran downstairs to the basement. Anthony and Mikey looked at Desi and me hopefully.

Desi laughed. "If Mikey's mom says it's ok, you boys can go too."

I nodded. "Go ahead." The boys scurried away before we could change our minds.

Lincoln and Beth returned, carrying a basketful of rolls. I grabbed one as she passed by me and tore off some pieces to give to Ella, who'd finished everything she'd had on the high chair tray.

"Where did the kids go?" Beth set the rolls down in front of Adam. "I wanted to ask them about school."

"I said they could be excused." Tania locked eyes with Beth.

"Oh." Beth busied herself with stacking the empty plates the kids had left behind. "Maybe with the kids gone, this is a good time to talk about you moving back up here."

Will suddenly became fascinated by his napkin and Tania threw her head back and stared at the ceiling. When her face leveled out, there was fire in her eyes and she said to Beth, "Not that it's any of your business, but we're not moving. We have lives back in Phoenix." She turned to Will. "Got that? We're not moving."

"Tania," he said, "maybe we could use a fresh start."

Beth watched their exchange intently.

"No." Tania threw her napkin on the table. "Maybe *you* could use a fresh start—without the girls and me." She sneered at Beth and walked out of the room, the front door slamming behind her.

Will leaned forward and ran his fingers through his hair. "Where did things go so wrong?"

"You'll be happier back home," Beth said firmly. "And it would be better for the girls too. If Tania can't see that, well ..."

Will looked at his mother. "She's my wife." He folded his napkin and stood.

Adam did the same. "How about we take a walk together, check out all of the changes to our old stomping grounds."

Will walked toward the front door. "Anything to get away from here."

When her sons were gone, Beth's eyes filled with tears. "I didn't mean to make him mad."

Desi took a deep breath. "Mom, you were awfully harsh on Tania. Not that she's my favorite person either, but Will's right—she's his wife."

Beth's lips quivered. "I just want what's best for him. Ever since he married her, he's seemed so unhappy, nothing like the old Will."

Lincoln scooted his chair closer to his wife and put his arm around her. "I'm sure he knows that you want the best for him."

The tension in the room was so thick and uncomfortable that I couldn't take it anymore. I picked up some of the serving dishes and carried them into the kitchen, setting them on the counter. Desi followed suit with the dirty plates and cups. Lincoln and Beth still hadn't moved. Lina and Ella stared at the tears streaming down their grandmother's face, fascinated by the unusual sight.

When we finished clearing the table, I said, "I'm going to check on Mikey, then sit in the living room until Adam gets back, ok?"

No one answered, so I went into the basement family room and checked on the boys. The kids had taken a plastic bowling set out of the toy cupboard and were pretending the long room was a bowling alley. Bella was sitting in a corner with her knees drawn up to her chest and her nose buried in a book.

"Strike!" Maya shouted when Anthony rolled the ball directly at the pins, knocking them all down. The girls seemed happy and I hoped that they hadn't overheard their parents arguing.

I went back upstairs to get Ella out of her high chair, but when I reached the dining room, Beth was holding her and didn't want to let go, so I escaped to the relative calm of the living room. Desi had curled up on an overstuffed chair and was checking something on her phone while Lina fussed in a baby swing nearby.

I wasn't sure if I should say something to her about the threat I'd received the day before. I'd placed both the doll and the note in a bag and stashed it under a seat in my car where no one would look. I probably should have told the police about it, but then I'd have to admit that I'd been doing a little sleuthing of my own. Desi and I had promised our husbands that we'd try to stay out of trouble, and if they got wind of what was in the plastic bag, they wouldn't be too happy.

"The boys are all right?" Desi asked, still staring at her phone. I decided not to tell her. If she didn't know about the threat, she wouldn't have the dilemma of whether or not to tell Tomàs about it.

"They're having the time of their lives with Will's girls." I may not have appreciated the girls' overabundance of energy, but the boys certainly did. "It's nice to see them playing with their cousins."

Desi looked up from her phone. "Well, they'll have a lot of chances to do that if Will moves up here."

"Do you think he will?"

She shrugged. "No idea. I can't get a read on him. Sometimes he acts like he loves Tania and then other times it seems like he despises her."

"I don't think he knows either." I plopped down on the sofa. My phone rang and I quickly picked it up, thinking it was Adam.

Anna Westen, the display read. My heart beat faster.

"Hi, Anna."

"Hi. Remember that thing you asked me about earlier?" she asked cryptically.

How could I forget? "Yes," I said tersely. Desi gave me an odd look.

"Well, if one of the subjects we spoke about happened to be a client of ours, they may have had a series of large transactions out of their bank accounts in the weeks before their death. Does the Calvado Group mean anything to you?"

The name sounded familiar. "Maybe?"

"I've never heard of it before, but they're hundreds of thousands of dollars richer now, thanks to a certain person." In a softer voice, she said, "I hate to think of someone scamming an elderly person. You're sure the police are working on this? If these transactions aren't on the up and up, I want to make sure whoever's behind the Calvado Group pays for this."

"I will. I hate it too," I said. "Thanks, Anna."

"No problem. Hey, if you want to get together for coffee after Christmas, let me know."

"I'd like that. Thanks for calling."

"Glad to be able to help. Talk to you later."

I hung up and set the phone down next to me.

"Who was that?" Desi asked. "It sounded serious."

"That was Anna Westen."

"Oh!" She sat upright on the couch. "Did she find anything out about those men?"

"She said that the client 'may' have had some big transfers recently to a company called the Calvado Group." I peered at her. "Have you heard of it?"

"No." She shook her head. "Wait. I might. It's tickling the back of my brain."

I stared at the bright, multi-colored lights on the

Christmas tree that Beth had set up in the corner, letting myself get lost in the glow. Where had I heard that name before? Oh!

I held my finger up. "Hold on." I rummaged around in my purse for the piece of paper I'd found in Mila's book. After a few false starts, I plucked it from the depths of my bag.

She'd written *Calvado Building*. I grabbed my phone and did an internet search for Calvado Building.

"Desi," I hissed, "the Calvado Building was that one that caught on fire in Seattle years ago and the floor collapsed under the firefighters. Four of them were killed."

"Oh. That's right. I knew I'd heard of it before." She stopped to think. "Do you think they're related?"

"They have to be." I held up the piece of paper I'd found in Mila's book. "What are the odds that I'd find this on Mila's desk and then the Calvado Group comes up now too?"

"True." She took the paper from me, rubbing her fingers across the words. "So Mila did find something out about the men being conned—and the wrong person found out she knew."

"Yeah. So now we just have to figure out who's behind the Calvado Group."

"I'll do some digging tomorrow," Desi said. "There has to be some official record of it on file with the state."

"Tomorrow's Saturday. I don't think you'll be able to find out much until Monday."

"Oh, yeah." Her face fell. "So, what now?"

"I'm not sure, but maybe we'll find out something else when we're at Ericksville Heights tomorrow for the Christmas party."

"A little spy work while we're serving cookies?" she asked.

"Something like that." The information in this case was trickling in, but not fast enough for my liking. It seemed like we kept getting little pieces of the puzzle, but nothing to glue them all together. I hoped I was right that we'd find out more the next day.

"It's only for the night." Adam lifted an extra blanket off the top shelf in our guest room. "Will doesn't want to stay at Mom and Dad's because he feels so much pressure from Mom to move up here. He really unloaded on me when we were out tonight." He put the blanket down on the bed and I helped him smooth it out. "It's funny. I always thought of him as being so together and now I find out that his life is crumbling around him."

I glanced at the hallway, but I didn't see or hear Will, who we'd left watching TV in the living room. "What did he say about Tania? Does he want to stay with her?"

I heard a noise in the hallway and went to check it out, but it was just Goldie. He came into the guest bedroom, turned around a few times, then curled up on the floor.

"He's so confused by everything that he doesn't know. I told him to sleep on it and see how he feels in the morning. Maybe if he's away from her and Mom, he'll be able to think more clearly."

"That makes sense." I tucked the bottom corner of the blanket under the mattress. "Your mom really hates Tania though. I've never seen her act like that before."

Adam sighed. "He probably wouldn't be too happy that I'm telling you this." He cast a furtive glance at the hallway and lowered his voice. "Right before they were married, Tania cheated on Will. He forgave her, but Mom found out about it and never has forgiven Tania for hurting her first-born son."

"Ouch. But still. I'm glad she doesn't hate me. She's tough when she wants to be." I shuddered, imagining again what my life would be like if I didn't have a good relationship with Beth.

"Me too." He smiled and came around to wrap his arms around me. "Promise if there's ever anything that's bothering you about our relationship that you'll tell me?"

"If you promise to never have a mid-life crisis and move us to an island B and B, yeah. I can do that." I laughed and kissed him. "Or if you do, let's talk about it first, ok?"

"I can agree to that." He glanced at the hall. "I'd better get back to Will. Can you make sure that Mikey's asleep? I put him to bed, but he seems pretty amped-up."

"Sure." I couldn't imagine not being amped-up after an evening with Will's girls. They were so full of energy that it was probably like being at a fascinating carnival for Mikey and Anthony. I had to admit, I liked seeing them in small doses, but I wasn't sure about having them move up here.

"Hey, before you go. Do you remember a fire at the Calvado Building in Seattle?"

"Yeah, the news covered it for days. One of the clients of my law firm owned the building and was blamed for the condition of the building."

"Who was it?" Adam was usually pretty close-mouthed about any of his clients, but I hoped he'd make an exception this time.

He regarded me carefully, as if weighing his options, then sighed. "I suppose it doesn't really matter now. We were the attorneys on record for his company. Harry Pearson owned the building. He always claimed that he didn't know that the conditions were that bad and I think he spent the rest of his life trying to make up for it as well as he could." He kissed me on the cheek. "See you later." He strode off toward the living room, with Goldie hot on his heels.

So Harry Pearson had owned the Calvado Building. I knew he was wrapped up in all of this, even if his son denied a connection. But how did that all fit into the rest of it—the investment scam and the possible murders of the three men, not to mention Mila?

19

The day of the Christmas party at the retirement home had arrived. It was scheduled for two o'clock, but I got there at noon to start setting up. I'd left Mikey at home with Adam, but Desi had come early to help me get things ready.

"All of the decorations are up in the Great Room," she said.

"Even the snowflakes that the elementary school made?" I'd found a stack of snowflakes in a box in Mila's office and decided that they'd add to the festive look.

"Yep." She laughed. "And everyone has their noses pressed to the doors, trying to see through those tiny windows what's going on in there." She sobered. "Seriously, Jill, it was so nice of you to do this for everyone here. I know Delilah is excited."

"Yeah. I wasn't sure about it at first, but it's grown on me. Delilah has too. I'm going to try to make time to see her every week after this."

"I get the feeling she doesn't have company often. I'll try to do the same and ask if Mom can stop by too." She picked up my notebook. "Is there anything else I can do right now?"

"You can start setting up the refreshments table. The kitchen prepared some light appetizers and a local women's club brought by at least twenty dozen cookies. We need to set up some of those longer tables there and put tablecloths on them. I think you can ask one of the men from maintenance to help you move it."

"Ooh. I hope Mabel Swanson was one of the women who made cookies. I've been dying to get my hands on her gingerbread cookie recipe. If she made them this year, maybe I can taste one and reverse engineer it."

I fought to keep from laughing. Desi's mind was never far from sweets. "Maybe." I looked at the list too. "I've got to get the Santa suit out of Alfred and Mila's office before our Santa arrives. I'll come help you when I'm done."

"Ok." She went off to find someone to help her move the tables and I went to Alfred's office.

Alfred had taken the day off, so I was surprised to see the light on under the door and hear someone moving around in his office, slamming the file cabinet closed. Unease stirred in the pit of my stomach. It was probably just Nurse Fluge getting some patient files out. Still, I approached the door and quietly pushed it open, peeking around the corner. The first thing that caught my eye was shiny silver streamers.

I flung it open. "Delilah? What are you doing in here?"

She stepped back quickly and stumbled. I managed to get to her before she could fall sideways.

She put her hand over her heart. "You startled me."

"I didn't expect anyone to be in here either." I stared at the open drawer containing the employee records. "Are you snooping?"

She blushed. "I'm trying to figure out what's going on around here. Goodness knows the police aren't doing anything about it." She nudged the drawer shut with her walker.

I frowned. "That's not entirely true."

"Oh, I know you weren't telling me the whole truth earlier," she said. "But you probably didn't want to upset me, right?"

She had me there.

"I'm a lot stronger than people give me credit for." She straightened her hunched back and gripped the handles of her walker.

"I'm not disputing that," I said carefully. "But Mila was killed for what she found out."

"I know. And someone needs to pay for that." She jutted her chin out. "I'm going to head back to my room now to freshen up before the party starts."

I watched her go, faster than I would have thought. *I want to be just like her when I'm old.*

I grabbed the Santa suit out of the corner and headed back to the kitchen. Now, not only did I have to worry about my own safety, but I'd also failed to keep Delilah out of the investigation and had her safety to worry about as well. Whoever had killed Mila needed to be found—and fast.

"Killer party, ma'am," a man in his twenties wearing a tie-dyed shirt said when I came to check on how things were going at their table. "Grandpa's really enjoying it."

I smiled. "Thanks. The community helped a bunch." I'd been impressed by the family turnout for the party and was now thankful that the local women's club had made so many cookies for it.

Santa would be coming in soon to sit by the fire and take pictures with the kids and the kids at heart. The round tables were full of people smiling and laughing together. By all accounts, the party was a roaring success.

But where was Delilah? I knew the party was important to her, so I'd expected to find her sitting at the front of the room with her daughter. I'd been to every table and she wasn't there. I knocked on her door, but there was no answer, so I checked to see if Desi had seen her.

"Delilah?" Desi wrinkled her face in thought. "No, you're right. I haven't seen her recently. I've been so busy that I didn't even realize she wasn't here. I talked to her earlier though, and I don't think her daughter was going to be able to make it after all."

"Oh, and she'd been looking forward to seeing her. That's too bad."

"Yeah, she was pretty broken up about it. She was supposed to go home with her daughter for Christmas too, and now she's stuck here."

That explained why she had been off in Alfred's office snooping in his files instead of spending time with her daughter and enjoying the festivities.

"I'll check for her in her room again." I went down the hall and stopped in front of Delilah's door, then knocked on it. There wasn't any answer.

"Delilah?" I called out. Still nothing. I hoped she was ok. The doorknob turned easily, and I swept my eyes over her small room and the open door to the bathroom. No Delilah.

I found Desi again.

"Is she ok?" Desi asked.

"I can't find her. She's not in her room. Do you think she

went outside or something?" It was below freezing, and the thought of her being out there alone was concerning.

"I'll ask one of her friends that I saw her talking with last week." Desi jetted off across the room, stopping at a table that was occupied by an elderly man and what looked to be his grandchildren. I saw him gesture in the direction of the door and my stomach lurched.

Desi returned a minute later. "He said he saw her head back to the kitchen."

"Oh, I'm so happy to hear that. Maybe she wanted to help with the party." I frowned, thinking about our discussion earlier. "I'd like to make sure she's ok though."

"Yeah. I want to make sure she's ok too. I feel awful about her daughter not coming today. I'll come with you to find her."

We walked back to the kitchen, but Delilah wasn't there. I asked around and none of the staff had seen her.

"Ok, what now?" I asked.

"Where else would she be?" Desi looked out the window and pointed to the back of the kitchen where there was an exterior door. "She could still have gone outside."

I ran to the window. "I don't see her on the lawn or in the gardens."

"We should go outside," Desi said. "What if she's hurt or something?"

We grabbed coats from where we'd stashed them in the kitchen and walked toward the back door. We were about to go outside when something silver in the corner caught my eye.

"Desi, stop."

"What? Do you see her?"

"No, but look at that." I pointed at Delilah's walker, standing forlorn in the corner of the mudroom area just inside the door. I had a sinking feeling about the abandoned walker.

"She must be around here somewhere. She wouldn't go far without that." Desi turned in a circle. "There." She pointed at a door that was open a crack. "Where does that go?"

"I don't know. I've only ever been in the kitchen and the public areas of Ericksville Heights. This place is old and probably has a rabbit warren of rooms."

"Well, there's only one way to find out." Desi opened the door and flipped on a light switch. "Hey, there are stairs here. I bet it goes to the basement."

I hadn't even known the building had a basement, but it made sense that they'd have one in a building this old. Even with the light on, it looked like a gaping hole, and I couldn't see the end of the staircase.

"Delilah?" I called down the stairs. No answer.

Desi tried too. "Delilah? Are you down there?"

"What if she fell down the stairs or something?" I asked. "We've got to go down there and find her."

Desi stared at the basement. "Are we sure she's not outside?"

"No, this was right next to her walker. If she'd gone outside, she would have taken it with. She couldn't have taken it down the stairs very easily."

She sighed. "Fine, let's go. But you're going first. This place is creepy."

"Ok, but wait." I ran to where I'd left my purse in the kitchen and retrieved the Maglite I kept in there.

I led the way down the stairs and we came out on an open space with a boiler furnace and a web of steam pipes.

"Wow," Desi said, looking up. "This place is massive."

"No kidding. At least you won't feel claustrophobic down here."

I stepped on something that stuck to my shoe and fought to get it off.

"What are you doing?" Desi asked. "You look like an electrocuted octopus."

"There's something sticking to my shoe," I grumbled. Finally I took it off and peeled off a cherry Life Savers.

"A Life Savers ..." Desi said in a breathy voice.

"Yeah. She's got to be down here." With renewed vigor, I shouted for Delilah again. "Which way do you think she went?"

"That way." Desi pointed straight ahead. "Look on the floor."

Another Life Savers.

"It's like she's leaving a trail for us." We were out of the dim light from the stairway and I switched on my flashlight, shining the bright beam ahead of us.

"Or for herself." Desi looked from side to side as we walked. "These hallways are getting narrower."

To our left were a series of doors. I pushed each of them open and shone the flashlight into them. Each of them was a small room that would barely fit a twin bed. All of them were empty—until we got to the fifth room.

"Shine the light into the corner of the room," Desi said.

I obeyed her and illuminated a small table that someone had been using as a desk. A pen and notepad sat on it and a corkboard hung over it.

"What is that on there?" she asked, pointing at the mess of papers tacked to the board. "It looks like a newspaper article."

We moved closer.

The front-page headline read, *4 firefighters die in Calvado Building fire, slumlord blamed for poor conditions.*

"Calvado." My eyes flickered across each item pinned to the corkboard. I pointed at another article. "Harry Pearson owned the building."

"What?" Desi moved closer to read it.

"I forgot to tell you. Adam told me Harry Pearson owned the Calvado Building." I turned away from the corkboard and turned the light toward the other end of the room.

"There's a duffle bag over here." The bag was unzipped and I spread it open. It was packed with clothing and a passport. With trepidation, I opened the passport and saw the unsmiling face of Nurse Fluge staring up at me. Diana Fluge Marice.

"Desi," I said urgently. "Who were the firefighters that were killed? Was one of them named Marice?"

She ran her finger over the pictures of each of the firefighters. "Yeah, Mark Marice. How did you know?"

I flipped the passport open to show her. "We need to find Delilah now."

20

"*I*'ll show you where she is," said a voice from the door. "I'm sure she'd love company." Nurse Fluge wacked the flat end of a firefighter's ax against the palm of her hand as she gave us a crazy smile, then flipped on a headlamp.

I froze like a deer in the headlights. As I'd feared, she had Delilah. *She'd better not have hurt her.*

"Uh ..." Desi said, her eyes roving wildly across the room.

I didn't see anything we could use as a weapon against Nurse Fluge either. The flashlight was too small to hurt anyone, so I casually stuck it in my coat pocket, hoping she wouldn't see me.

Maybe if we could get her to talk, we'd have more time to find something useful.

Desi must have thought of the same thing. "If your plan all along was to kill Harry Pearson, why kill those other men and take their money too?"

She shrugged. "I needed to finance my trip to Brazil somehow. It might surprise you, but being a nurse at a retirement home doesn't bring home the big bucks, especially this place, but when I found out Harry Pearson was living here, I couldn't resist the opportunity to get close to him."

"Did you kill Mila?" I asked, inching closer to the desk.

She sneered. "She asked me too many question about the medications that Lenny and Albert were taking. Then she told me that the residents suspected something was wrong. I had to get rid of her."

"But why have her hang to death?" Desi asked.

"Well, that wasn't my intention. I'd planned a simple heart attack to make it appear that she'd died of natural causes, but when I was making my rounds that night, I saw her come in the side door. She was stumbling a little and I could tell she'd been drinking. When I saw her grab the ladder from the maintenance shed and drag it over to the back of the building, I knew it was too good to be true." She laughed. "I waited until she was messing around with the lights and grabbed it out from under her. I thought she'd fall, but the lights caught her around her neck." She shrugged. "It all worked out in the end."

"Except the part about the police figuring out it wasn't an accident," Desi said.

Nurse Fluge scrunched up her face. "That was unfortunate."

"Maybe you shouldn't have moved the ladder," Desi said helpfully. "If you'd left it there, they'd never have known."

While she had her attention, I felt blindly around to my right, hoping there would be something I could use against our captor. Nothing.

Nurse Fluge smacked her hand with the ax again. "Let's go."

We didn't move.

"Now," she shouted.

Desi and I inched toward the door and she let us move past her into the hallway, but blocked our way back to the stairs. She had us march down the hall until we came to the last door in the hallway.

"Go in."

I put my fingers on the old-fashioned round doorknob. The scarred metal was cold beneath my hand when I twisted the knob. It squeaked as I eased it open. Nurse Fluge's headlamp revealed a room that was slightly larger than the room with the desk.

"Sometime this year," Nurse Fluge said. When we didn't move, she pushed first me, then Desi into the room and slammed the door shut, locking it from the outside with a key.

"Jill?" Desi said, her voice sounding far away in the pitch black. "Do you still have the flashlight?"

"Yeah. Hold on." I flipped on the Maglite and swept it across the room. We were locked in a ten by ten space with a wooden storage rack on one side and a few bins along another wall. The walls were made of stone and mortar. The light hit a pile of clothing in the corner nearest the rack and we moved closer.

"That's Delilah." I could taste the fear in my mouth. I turned the light to a wide focus and let it shine upwards, illuminating much of the room.

"Is she ...?" Desi said, frozen in place.

"I don't know." I knelt down beside the elderly woman and felt for a pulse on her neck. "She's alive." I ran the light over her. "She's got a goose egg on the back of her head that's going to hurt when she wakes up, but otherwise looks ok."

"Other than being locked inside a cement room in the Basement of Doom?"

I shrugged. "It's better than the alternative. Besides, maybe someone will find us down here."

Desi gave me an incredulous look. "Seriously? Who's going to look for us down here?"

"Maybe Nurse Fluge will come back." I was trying to think positively, but everything I came up with fell flat.

"Who are you kidding? She'll be halfway to Canada by now. And why would you want her to come back anyway? Not that it matters. We're dead. Face it." Desi paced the room, tugging on the doorknob until her fingers turned red, then slumped down against the wall. "Blueberry scones, chocolate donuts, cheese Danishes."

Her claustrophobia was kicking in. If we didn't get out of here soon, she'd be a basket case. I pulled my phone out of my jacket pocket. As I'd expected, there was no service in the basement, but maybe it would come in handy later.

Next to us, Delilah stirred.

Jarred out of her trance, Desi crawled across the floor to sit down beside her and stroked her forehead. "It's ok."

Delilah tried to sit up, but only succeeded in slumping against the wall. "My head." She touched the back of her head and her fingers came back bloody. "Oh my." She pushed herself up to a seated position. "Nurse Fluge. I followed her down here and she hit me with something. But where are we now?"

"No clue," Desi said. "Somewhere at the far end of the basement. We followed the trail of Life Savers you left behind and then she got us."

Delilah frowned. "I'm sorry, girls. I never meant for you to get hurt. I dropped the candy on the ground so I could find my way back if I got lost."

Desi put her hand on Delilah's arm. "Don't worry about it. If it hadn't been for your Life Savers, we'd never have found you."

The elderly woman nodded feebly, then looked at the walls. "It looks like a cellar or something." She slowly turned her head to check out the rest of the room. "This must have been a storage cellar."

I picked up the flashlight to see if there was anything of use in the bins. Nothing but dirt. "Nothing good."

"Well, I always said I'd be happy to die in this house. I didn't mean like this though. But I'm old and if it's my time, it's my time." Delilah looked at us. "You girls are so young though. You have families and whole lives left to live."

I bit my lip to stop from crying. Images of my kids and Adam flashed through my mind. Adam would look for me, I knew he would—but could he find us?

I took a deep breath.

"Someone is going to find us," I said firmly, trying to convince myself as well as the others that we'd be all right. "We just need to be patient." A slight fear that Nurse Fluge would come back and kill us ran through my mind, but I suspected she was long gone.

Desi looked at me with skepticism but went along with it. "Delilah, why don't you tell us more about what Ericksville was like when you were young. I'd like to hear more about this building too."

Delilah leaned against the wall. "Well, like I told you before, it was built in 1902 as the Ericksville Heights hotel."

"It must have been a gorgeous hotel." Thinking about the hotel in its heyday gave me a little comfort.

"It was," Delilah said. "Or so my mother told me. When she was a kid, everyone was in awe of the hotel. People from all over the world stayed here—wealthy people, famous people, it was even rumored that a president spent the night here."

She regaled us with stories about her mother working at the hotel as a chambermaid while she was a teenager. "But then the Great Depression hit and people stopped coming. The hotel was sold and the new owners, who were rumored to be rumrunners, turned the hotel into a sanatorium for tuberculosis patients."

"I wonder what it was like to live in the era of Prohibition." Desi pulled her knees up to her chest. "You always hear about the speakeasies and such. It must have been so glamorous."

"Do you really think the owners were rumrunners?" I asked Delilah.

Her smile gleamed in the meager light. "I know they were. My mother was a beautiful twenty-year-old when the hotel changed hands, and for a while, she dated one of the young men who worked in the sanatorium, ostensibly as a driver. She soon learned what he really did for a living."

"Wow." Desi stared at her wide-eyed. "I bet this was one of their storerooms."

"I wouldn't doubt it. They'd have needed somewhere to keep the liquor," Delilah said. "You know, I heard stories about there being a speakeasy in downtown Ericksville, right where that little curio shop is on Second Street. I've always wondered if it was real." Delilah proceeded to tell us more about the history of Ericksville. Before I knew it, another hour had passed. Her skill at weaving tales of the past had almost made me forget we were locked in the very cellar that we were romanticizing.

I stood, running my hand over the rough stonework. If these walls could talk. I checked my watch. We'd been missing from the party for a couple of hours already and no one had found us.

"What time is it?" Desi asked.

I told her and she sighed. "They should have been looking for us by now."

"I'm sure they are." I laughed. "Tomàs probably has every cop in a hundred mile radius looking for you."

She tried to smile. "And maybe all of the Coast Guard's boats too."

I pictured the Coast Guard searching the bluffs below the retirement home, searching every nook and cranny. Inspiration struck and I ran my fingers along the wall.

"You're not going to be able to dig us out of here with your fingers," Desi said.

"I know." I continued what I was doing until I reached the wall with the storage unit. In Nancy's house, they'd hidden a door to the basement behind an armoire. Maybe there was something behind this one. "Desi, help me move this?"

"Why? Are you planning on stabbing the walls with pieces of wood you break off of there?"

"Nope."

With much huffing and puffing, she helped me ease it to the left. She stood up and rubbed her back. "At least I'm warmer now from all that exercise."

I took the light and examined the wall. I could just make out a thin rectangle that was different from the rest of the masonry.

"Seriously, what are you doing?" Desi asked. "We're not in the South, so there's probably not a branch of the Underground Railroad here."

"No, there's not." I pressed on the stones until a particularly long one gave way and the door swung open.

21

*D*elilah pushed herself up from the ground and walked shakily over to the hole in the wall. "Why didn't I think of that?"

"I'm feeling a little left out here," Desi said, pouting.

"It's a rumrunner's tunnel. That's how they smuggled the alcohol into the sanatorium."

Her eyes widened. "So all we have to do is follow it out?"

"I don't know." There were cobwebs hanging from every crevice in the tunnel, but the wooden support beams looked surprisingly sturdy for being ninety years old. "I don't know if it's safe. Or the other entrance could have been boarded up after all of these years."

Delilah nudged me aside and took the flashlight, examining the wooden beams. "It's good."

"How do you know?" Desi asked.

"I'm a carpenter's daughter. I know good woodworking and this was good woodwork. It'll hold." As if to prove her point, she moved past me and entered the tunnel, holding on to the sides to keep her balance without the walker.

Desi sighed. "I'll go first. Maybe that will keep the claustrophobia at bay."

She stepped in front of Delilah, who handed her the flashlight without complaint. I brought up the rear as we made our way along the tunnel. It seemed to slope slightly downward, but nothing significant. Other than some broken bottles, the dirt path was fairly clear of debris.

I still wasn't sure about the safety of the tunnel, but we didn't have much choice. Delilah seemed to be doing ok and was using the sides of the tunnel for support. After we'd been walking for a while, a metal door blocked our path.

"Do you think it goes out to the water?" I asked.

Delilah answered me. "Maybe. Or it could go to another house even. We'll have to find out."

"If it even still opens." I was more nervous now than I'd been all evening. If this didn't work out, we were out of options. There was no way I could pull another exit out of thin air.

Desi looked at me. "Here goes nothing." She pulled on the door handle and nothing happened. She tugged on it again and it creaked open a hair. "I think it's stuck on something."

I scanned the ground below the door. Over the years, dirt had come down from the tunnel's roof and formed a door stop. I kicked the dirt aside with the toe of my good black flats. "Try it now."

This time, the door opened about a foot. We gave Delilah the flashlight and she moved to the side to allow us room. Desi and I both yanked on it with our full body weight and managed to create a gap big enough for us to fit through. I gulped the fresh air scented with recent rain and stepped out the door into the pitch black night.

"Where are we?" I whispered.

"I don't know," Desi whispered back.

"Why are you girls talking so quietly?" Delilah asked, as she aimed the light ahead of us.

"I don't know. It seems spooky out here." I spun around in a slow circle. "We're in the woods I think."

"I hear the water close by though." Desi cocked her head to the side.

"I bet we're in the gulch that runs along the side of the Ericksville Heights grounds." Delilah ran the flashlight along the trees in front of us. "See the slope? The water is that way."

"Hey, maybe my phone works now." I pulled it out, but still had no bars. "Maybe we can get a signal down by the water where it's more open."

Desi looked up the hill. "Better than going up."

She was right. The foliage was thick and I wasn't sure we could safely make it up to the top in the dark.

I glanced at Delilah. "Will you be ok out here without your walker?" Not that her walker would be of much use with all the brush.

She stepped forward tentatively. "I think I'll be fine. I keep the walker around most of the time in case my leg gives out, but it's been better lately."

We started down the hill with Desi in the lead, then Delilah, then me, much as we had in the tunnel.

"Ouch," Delilah cried out. She tumbled to the ground and grabbed her foot.

We stopped immediately. "Are you ok?" Desi asked.

Delilah tested her foot and ankle by rotating them in small circles. "I think so."

We helped her up and she winced.

"Do you think you can make it to the water?" I asked.

She nodded. "I'm tougher than I look."

Desi laughed. "I don't think we doubted that for a minute. You've been through a lot today."

We climbed over fallen trees and rocks that the recent rain had made slick. Desi and I took turns helping Delilah, and we soon made it to the beach.

The tide must have been out, because there was a stretch of sand showing above the water. I didn't see any boats out on the water, but the sparkling lights of Willowby Island across the way were a welcome sight. Delilah sat down on a log to rest while I tried my phone again. I had bars of service!

With trembling fingers, I punched the buttons. When the emergency dispatcher answered, I told her we were at the bottom of the gulch next to Ericksville Heights and we had an elderly woman with us who wouldn't be able to walk out of there.

"I'm sorry, ma'am, but did you say you had an elderly woman with you?" the dispatcher asked.

"Yes. It's a long story. We were kidnapped by a nurse at Ericksville Heights Retirement Home—Diana Fluge Marice. She may be on the way to Brazil. The police need to find her —she tried to kill us. Tell them Desi Torres is with us. Her husband Tomàs is a police officer for Ericksville." I gave her the rest of our names and the other information that she requested.

When I was finished, the dispatcher said in a calm voice, "The police and aid crew are on their way."

I hung up and sat down on the cold sand with my back against the log. We'd been running on pure adrenaline for so long that I hadn't had a chance to internalize any of what had happened. We'd just been locked in an over one-hundred-year-old cellar and escaped via a tunnel built by people smuggling rum into the country. I'd thought the biggest thing that might happen that day would be to find out more clues about Mila's murder. How wrong I'd been.

"Is that a boat?" Desi pointed to a bright light in the water. I peered at it as it came closer to the beach. Sure enough, Ericksville had deployed their small police boat to help us.

The rescue workers beached the boat and an EMT jumped out, carrying a bag. "Is someone hurt?"

Desi and I pointed at Delilah. I was half-afraid she wouldn't admit that there was anything wrong with her, but her ankle must have been bothering her more than she let on because she let him examine her.

He signaled to the boat driver. "She's ok, but I'll need help getting her into the boat." He turned to us. "Are you two ok if we take her back to the marina? There wasn't enough room on the boat for the police to come with us, but they're waiting back on shore. We'll come right back for you."

"We're fine," Desi said. "Go. Get Delilah somewhere warm and safe."

He set a battery-powered lantern on the beach. "We'll be back soon."

The boat roared away from the gulch and disappeared around the corner.

Desi and I looked at each other over the white light emanating from the lantern.

"Well, this has been an interesting day," she said.

"No kidding." I looked out at the water. "What do you think Tomàs and Adam are going to say?"

"They're probably not going to be too happy. But it genuinely wasn't our fault this time. We were trying to find an elderly woman." She smiled. "Plus, Will's no longer a suspect now—or at least he won't be once we have a chance to tell the police what happened. And my mom never found out that he was a murder suspect."

"Maybe they'll have been so worried about us that they won't care." I looked at my phone, just now realizing I could call my husband and let him know we were ok. I dialed his number and waited for it to ring, but he answered as soon as the call connected.

"Jill? What's going on? Are you ok?" Adam asked. "Tomàs called and said to come down to the marina—that something had happened to you and Desi, but that you were fine. I've was so worried when you didn't come home."

"We'll be at the marina soon. We're fine, don't worry. I'll tell you all about it when I see you."

A bright light came at us on the water. The boat had returned.

"Adam, I have to go. See you in a few minutes."

Desi and I climbed into the boat and got ourselves situated with life jackets, then the driver took off. We jetted across the water, leaving a white wake behind us. It was faster than I'd thought to get to the marina and we were soon passing the Ericksville Lighthouse and the Boathouse. My heart quickened at the familiar sights, places that I never thought I'd see again when Nurse Fluge had locked us in the cellar.

The driver pulled up to a dock at the marina and tied up, then reached his hand out to help me up. I grasped it and stepped onto the dock. I stood there for a moment while he helped Desi disembark, my legs shaking. He led us down the dock and up the ramp to the marina office, where the police were waiting for us. An ambulance was parked in the parking lot and Delilah was sitting in the back of it with a blanket wrapped around her shoulders. We'd made it back alive.

"Jill!" Adam shouted as he raced over to me and drew me to him. "I was so worried."

I buried my head in his chest, happy to have his arms wrapping me in safety. I tipped my head up.

"Where are the kids?"

"I dropped them off with my parents. My mom only let me leave after I promised that I'd call her as soon as I could confirm you and Desi were safe." He looked around the parking lot. "There's Desi with Tomàs." He dialed his mother and told her we were both safe.

The police had given Adam and me a moment alone while they were talking with Desi, but now they beckoned for me to come over to them. Desi and I told them all about Nurse Fluge's schemes and what had happened to the three of us.

The lead police officer raised her eyebrows. "You're saying that this nurse caught you in the basement when you went looking for Mrs. Brown? And she locked you in the cellar?"

We nodded.

She talked into her radio and turned back to us. "They're looking for her and they'll search the basement too. I can't believe you escaped through a tunnel into the gulch." She shook her head. "I've heard rumors that there were tunnels in this area, but I never believed they were true."

"Me neither," said Desi. "Delilah had been telling us about the history of the building, and Jill thought to look behind a storage rack in the basement for a hidden door."

I nodded. "We were lucky the tunnel hadn't caved in over all of these years." I thought about the rack. I wouldn't have thought to check back there if I hadn't seen the armoire in Nancy's pantry. This wasn't the first time something she'd done had ended up saving me.

"You certainly were lucky." She snapped her notepad shut. "Ok, you're free to go now. We'll notify you if we need any other information." She walked away, and Desi and I just stood there for a moment.

"What now?" I asked. "I wonder how the Christmas party went?"

"Seriously, you're worried about that now?" Desi asked. "There are more important things to worry about, like dinner. I'm starving."

"Maybe we can convince Tomàs and Adam to take us to the diner before we go home."

"Sounds good to me."

22

"How are there this many presents?" Adam's arms were full of brightly wrapped Christmas gifts that were bound for his family's Christmas Eve get together.

"Well, we bought one gift for each adult and two for each kid. There are five adults and seven kids. You do the math." I picked up a present that had fallen on the ground. "I guess we don't need this one."

I placed Tania's present on the kitchen counter to be dealt with later.

"Still, that seems like a lot," he grumbled.

"Stop complaining, you didn't have to shop for them."

"True." He smiled at me as he walked through the open front door.

While he was packing them into the car, I ran through my checklist again. Presents, veggie platter, fudge. We were good to go.

When we arrived at Beth and Lincoln's house, Beth met us on the front walkway.

I got out of the car and she ran over to hug me.

"I can't believe what happened to you and Desi. And Delilah too."

"Me neither." Although it had only happened the day before yesterday, the whole event was like a dream in my mind, one that I wasn't quite sure had actually happened. The scratches on my leg burned in the cold air, reminding me that it hadn't been a dream.

"Well, I'm glad you're both ok." She looked at Adam, who was fumbling with an armload of presents. "Do you need help with those?"

"No, I'm fine. Help Jill with the kids." He walked up to the house and nudged the door open that Beth had left slightly ajar.

She freed Mikey from his car seat and I lifted Ella out of hers. Together, we entered the house.

It hadn't been that long since I'd been there for the last family dinner, but Beth had been doing some serious decorating in honor of Christmas Eve. The tree had been there before, but the decorations on the hearth were new, as were the neat line of ceramic houses on the windowsill. The aroma of turkey filled the air, mixing with the scent of the fresh pine tree. This was what Christmas smelled like.

I looked at Adam, who'd stacked the gifts under the tree. "Can we get a real tree next year?"

He shrugged. "Sure, honey. I thought you didn't want to deal with having one."

"I don't, but I want the kids to grow up knowing what they smell like."

He gave me an odd look that turned into a smile.

"Auntie Jill!" Maya said as she came upstairs wearing a fancy green velvet party dress. "Did you bring me a present?"

"Maya," Beth admonished. "You shouldn't ask things like that."

"Oh, all right." She moved closer to me and whispered, "But did you?"

"Yes," I whispered back as I tried not to laugh. The girls were starting to grow on me as I got used to their high energy levels.

"Mommy went back home," Maya said, suddenly serious.

I hugged her. "I know, honey. I bet she misses you lots and lots."

"She does." Maya's voice held the certainty that only a child could feel. "But we're going to celebrate Christmas together when we get back home too."

"That's great." I smiled at her. "Two Christmases will be awesome."

"Yeah!" Maya's lips formed a wide grin and then she ran downstairs to join her sisters and Mikey.

"We're here," Desi sang out as the door opened.

"And we brought gifts," Tomàs said in a less cheerful tone. "Way too many of them."

Adam shot me a "told you so" look and said, "Let me help you with those. I've become quite an expert in being a present sherpa myself." He grabbed the top half of Tomàs's stack and moved them to the tree.

Anthony left his parents and ran off downstairs. Lina was asleep in her carrier, so Desi set her next to the couch where we could keep an eye on her and went back outside. A few minutes later, she came back inside, but she wasn't alone.

I stood from the couch to greet the new guest at the front door. "Delilah!" I hugged her. "I didn't know you were coming tonight, but I'm so glad that you're here." Desi and I guided her over to the couch and then Desi went into the kitchen to find her mom.

"Desi invited me. I hope it's ok?" She looked around the room as she settled down into the couch pillows.

"It's more than ok. We're happy to have you, but I'm warning you, the kids can be quite loud."

"That's ok. It's been years since I had the chance to see little kids at Christmas."

"How are you feeling today? We saw you with the EMTs when we first got off of the boat, but then they whisked you away."

"Oh, that." She waved it off. "They took me to the hospital to get checked out, but released me later that night. There wasn't anything wrong with me that a good night's rest couldn't fix." She rotated her ankle to prove her point.

Through the open doorway between the kitchen and the dining room, I heard Beth greet Desi like she hadn't seen her in years. A few minutes later, Desi joined Delilah and me in the living room.

"You'll be happy to know that the police caught Nurse Fluge last night when she tried to buy a plane ticket to Brazil," she said.

"They did?" I asked. "When did you find out?"

"They called Tomàs and told him right before we came over here."

"That's a relief," Delilah said. "That woman was pure evil. Those poor men."

"What do you think will happen to Chas Pearson?" I asked Desi.

"Tomàs didn't say. I assume that now that they have her in custody, they'll start gathering evidence of her scams. We don't even know if Chas Pearson was aware of the financial losses his father experienced prior to death. For all we know, he could be completely innocent."

"I'd be willing to bet he's not," I said. "He may not have helped Nurse Fluge dupe his father out of money, but he must have known it happened—he just didn't care. Getting control of his father's finances was more important to him than righting a wrong."

Delilah nodded. "I don't think he's innocent either. From what you've told me about him, he would have known if money was missing."

"Well, if that's true, I'm sure the police will figure it out." Desi picked up Lina, who'd begun to fuss.

Will and Adam came back in the room and Delilah fawned over them, telling them what handsome young men they'd grown up to be. After dinner, Beth put a spread of desserts out on the dining room table that would make a sweets shop owner swoon.

"You know there's not that many of us, right, Mom?" Adam asked.

Beth glanced at Will's girls, who were in the corner of the living room, happily munching away at the fudge I'd brought and the Christmas cookies and cakes that she'd made. "I wanted it to be special for the girls. It must be hard for them to not have their mother here this year."

"I know, Mom." Adam snaked his arm around her shoulders and squeezed her to him for a moment. "Oh! I think I hear Ella out there." He walked off to the living room to check on her.

Will was engrossed in a conversation with Delilah and Desi, so I took the opportunity to ask Beth about Tania.

"Do you know what's going on with Tania? I knew she wasn't going to be here, but you didn't say anything about whether that's permanent or not."

Beth sighed. "I don't want to get too into it, but I think they're separating, at least for the time being."

"That's rough, especially at Christmas."

"It is." She looked at me. "This hasn't been the easiest of holiday seasons. When Tomàs called to tell me that you and Desi had been kidnapped, but were ok, it really threw me for a loop. I can't believe I almost lost the two of you." She wrapped her arms around me. "You're like a daughter to me. You know that, right?"

I smiled. "I feel the same way."

"Let's go out to the living room to join everyone, ok?"

Everyone was finishing up their desserts and I gathered the dirty plates to stick in the dishwasher.

"Presents time!" Beth announced.

The kids cheered and rushed to the Christmas tree.

"Which of you is going to be the Christmas elf?" Lincoln asked with his camera in hand.

"Me!" Mikey jumped up and wildly waved his hand in the air.

Lincoln laughed. "I think you're going to need an assistant elf who can read names.

"I'll do it," Bella said shyly. She stood from the floor, the skirt of her sparkly blue party dress floating in the air as she rose.

They handed out presents to everyone and it was a mad dash to open them. When everything was open and the floor was littered with wrapping paper, Beth clapped her hands. "In honor of having so many members of our family here this year to share in the holidays, I'd like us all to go around and say what we're grateful for this year."

The kids groaned.

"Do we have to?" whined Claire, who was bouncing on

her knees. Her grandmother fixed her eyes on her and she sat back down.

We went around the room, each of us saying what we were grateful for. When it reached Beth, she said, "I'm grateful to have my family here for Christmas and that they're all safe." She laughed. "And that none of them are currently murder suspects."

Desi's jaw dropped. "You knew?"

Beth raised an eyebrow. "Of course I knew. You don't think someone would mention to me that Will was suspected of murder?"

I guess I hadn't needed to be worried about keeping it from her because she'd known all along.

"Mom, why didn't you say anything to me?" Will asked.

She shrugged. "I figured you didn't want to tell me for some reason." She smiled at him. "And from now on, I'm keeping out of your personal life."

"Now that is something to be grateful for," Lincoln said. Beth slugged him on the arm, but he just pulled her close and kissed the top of her head.

We all know you only want us to be happy, Mom," Will said.

"I do," she said.

Will came over and hugged her. "Thanks, Mom."

"Enough of this mushy stuff," Desi said. "I want to see Dad try on his new tie."

Lincoln owned enough ties to wear a different one every day of the year and I think he was the rare father who actually appreciated getting one as a gift. He turned away from us and carefully knotted the tie around his neck then turned back around.

"What do you all think?"

We all started laughing when Rudolph's nose flashed on and off, highlighting the reindeer's goofy grin.

"It's perfect," I said.

And it was—well, perfectly the Andrews family. Sometimes kooky, sometimes serious, but always protective of their own. After a night with them, I couldn't wait to see what Christmas Day with my family would bring.

CHAPTER 23

I picked my parents up at the airport early on Christmas morning. Becky wouldn't be in until afternoon as she was driving up from her home in Portland. Mikey had wanted to open his Christmas stocking as soon as he woke up, but I made him promise to wait for us to get back from the airport. Adam had taken the stocking and hidden it to help him keep his promise.

"How was the flight?" I asked my parents as I helped them pull their bags off of the conveyor belt at baggage claim. Hundreds of people were crammed into the small area and I had to fight to stay upright as people dragged multiple suitcases tied together behind them.

"Good," my mom said. "Not too much turbulence." She hitched up the long strap of her purse over her shoulder and selected a small bag on rollers to carry.

"Beats driving across the mountain pass at this time of year." My father grabbed a large olive green suitcase and set it on the ground. "I remember one time when we got stuck on I-90 for three hours waiting for them to do avalanche control." He shuddered. "Never again."

"Well, I'm glad you're here. The kids have been looking forward to seeing you." I extended the handle on the remaining bag and motioned to a door at the far end of Sea-Tac airport. "This place is a madhouse today. I had to park pretty far away because I couldn't find anything closer."

We walked out to the car, making idle chitchat as we towed their roller suitcases behind us. When we were seated in the car, my mother asked from the backseat, "So what's this I hear about you and Desi getting stuck in a tunnel or something?"

I cringed. After how upset they'd been when I'd been in danger at Halloween, I'd hoped she wouldn't find about what had happened at Ericksville Heights. I peeked at her in the rearview mirror before I merged onto the freeway. "How did you find out?"

"Beth and I do talk, you know. But I shouldn't have to find something like that out from someone else." She narrowed her eyes at me.

"We worry about you," my father said. "It seems like you keep getting into these scrapes."

"Eh, it's no big deal. Desi and I got stuck in a basement and had to get out via a tunnel. We're fine now." I peeked at her again. Had she bought it? How much had Beth told her?

Judging by the frown on her face, she hadn't found my explanation convincing. Maybe it was time to change the subject.

"It's nice that Becky is able to come up for Christmas this year," I said. "I missed seeing her last year."

"She's had a rough year," Mom said. "I think she really needs her family around her right now. She seemed pretty down last time we were in Portland to see her."

Becky hadn't confided in me much and all I knew was that her husband had left her a few months ago. Now that the holidays were almost over and work was easing up, I hoped I'd be able to spend some quality time with her. We'd been close as kids, but our lives now were very different and I sometimes had a difficult time relating to her.

"How are the kids doing?" Mom asked. "Is Mikey still enjoying preschool? Did Ella get any more teeth? You've been so busy lately that I haven't had a chance to catch up on everything."

"Sorry. Things have been crazy at work with all of the Christmas parties." That and almost getting killed.

I told them all about what Mikey was up to in school and the cute things Ella had done that week. Soon, we were pulling up to our driveway in Ericksville. Adam had turned the Christmas lights back on and the house looked cheery and warm, with smoke puffing out of the chimney.

We went inside and I got my parents situated in our guest bedroom, then we let Mikey open his Christmas stocking. Santa had left stockings for Adam, Ella, and me, as well as my parents because he must have known they'd be there for Christmas. Santa knows everything, after all.

We were all sitting down to lunch when there was a knock at the door. Goldie barked and trotted over to the door. I checked to see who it was, then pushed Goldie out of the way so I could open it fully. My sister Becky stood on the steps. I smiled and pulled her in for a hug. "It's good to see you sis."

"You too." She pulled away from me. "Now, where are my favorite niece and nephew? I thought Mikey would be out here waiting for me."

"He probably would have if I'd let him." I grinned and shouted into the house, "Mikey! Aunt Becky's here."

He ran to the door and attached himself to her before she had even crossed the threshold.

"I love you too, buddy." My sister stepped into the room and removed her jacket, hanging it on the hook inside the door. "Brr. It's cold out there." Goldie sniffed at the jacket. "You can smell my cat, can't you?" she asked as she patted his head before walking into the kitchen.

"Hi, honey." Mom stood and embraced Becky. "I'm so glad you were able to come this year."

"Me too." Becky sat down at the table and smiled at everyone. She grabbed a scoopful of tuna salad and plopped it down on a piece of whole grain and nut bread. "This looks good. I wasn't hungry this morning when I left home and I didn't want to stop for food on the drive, so I'm starving now."

It was nice having my sister around again and filled me with hope that our relationship would be closer in the future. My phone buzzed and I checked it. Someone had e-mailed my personal account. On Christmas?

My good mood dissolved when I read the message. "Oh, great."

"What is it?" Adam asked.

"Our babysitter has decided to stay home for the semester because her father is ill and she wants to take care of him." I sighed. "Now what are we going to do?" I hastily added, "I mean, I'm glad that she's able to do that for him, but it's unfortunate for us."

Becky put her sandwich down on her plate. "You know, I might have a solution for that."

"Really? What?" I peered at her. "Do you know of someone in the area who's looking for a job?" Finding a babysitter hadn't been easy. I'd interviewed several candidates and only one had met my standards.

"Yeah. Me."

My mother's face lit up. "You're going to move up to Seattle? That would be wonderful. I could visit both of you in one trip."

"Not so fast, Mom, I haven't decided yet. I'm considering going back to school to become an elementary school teacher, but most of it is online until I get to the student teaching part of it." Becky looked at me. "What do you think?"

"I think you'd make a wonderful teacher," I said. "I'm surprised you aren't one already. You love kids and they love you. We'd love to have you around and for you to babysit the kids. That would be amazing."

"Following in our educator footsteps," my father said proudly.

"But what about your house?" I asked. "You worked so hard to build your tiny home. Are you going to sell it?" When she'd built the home the year before, she hadn't stopped talking about every part of the building process. I'd thought she was crazy until I'd seen how cute it was in person. As adorable as it was, however, I couldn't picture myself living there without going crazy, much less having two people living in the small space. I half wondered if that was one of the reasons for the breakup between Becky and her husband.

"That's the beauty of a tiny home. I can take it with me." She eyed Adam first, then me. "Actually, that's another thing I wanted to talk to you about. I was hoping I could park it in back of your house. It doesn't take up much space."

I froze. Did I want a tiny home in my backyard? Would the city even allow it? Most importantly, how did I feel about having my sister practically living with us?

She laughed. "I know. It's a lot. You don't have to decide now, but let me know so I can start making plans."

"We will," Adam said. "There are some things Jill and I

will need to talk about and we'll need to check with the town to see if it's even legal to have a tiny home on our property."

"Of course." She beamed at us. "I'd love to see my niece and nephew more often, but real estate is so expensive up here that I don't think I'd be able to afford an apartment while I attend school."

"We'll think about it and let you know." I smiled at her.

We spent the rest of the afternoon playing board games, singing Christmas carols in funny voices, and watching *It's a Wonderful Life*.

For dinner, my mother prepared our customary Christmas ham, which we ate with boiled new potatoes, green bean casserole, and a Jell-O fruit salad. My family usually had mincemeat and pecan pies for dessert, but Adam had insisted that Christmas wouldn't be complete without a chocolate cream pie. I'd half-heartedly fought with him over it because I didn't want to end up with pie leftovers hanging around the house and add to the five pounds I'd already gained this season, but I'd bought one from the grocery store and stuck it in the fridge for later. I didn't tell him because I didn't want to let him know how much I was looking forward to it, but I saved room at dinner for a big helping of chocolate pie. I mean, it was chocolate—how was I supposed to resist that?

After dinner, we exchanged gifts. I'd found a backpacker's espresso machine at the outdoors store and wrapped it up for Becky.

She unwrapped it and set it in front of her.

"Do you like it?" I asked anxiously.

"I do. I've been wanting one of these. I hate waking up and not having good coffee when I'm out hiking. I saw someone use one of these last time I went and was envious."

"I'm glad it will be useful for you." I'd gone back and forth on what to get her and was relieved that she liked it.

"You know, I'm sorry I put you on the spot earlier. If you don't want me living in your backyard, feel free to say so. I just thought it would benefit both of us—I'd get a cheap place to live and you'd get a live-in babysitter."

"I know. I'm not upset with you, but it's something Adam and I will have to talk about, ok?"

"Ok." She smiled at me, then crawled over to where Mikey was setting up a complicated race track that he'd received from my parents. She pointed at a piece of track and then at another, helping him to figure out where things went.

Later that night, with Ella sleeping in our room in a Pack 'n Play because Becky had her room, Adam and I had a chance to discuss Becky's proposition.

"What do you think, honey?" He peered at me.

"She's my sister. What do *you* think?"

"I think it might be a good idea. We've been so stressed about finding childcare that it's starting to take a toll on the family. And she's so good with the kids. We could leave them with her and know they were in good hands." He sat down on the bed and buttoned up his pajama top.

"But it would be another adult living here. Are we sure we want that? She'd probably be in the house all the time." Becky and I were so different that I wasn't sure what it would be like to have her here on a long-term basis. While my husband had often accused me of over-planning every-thing, Becky was the exact opposite—a go-with-the-flow kind of person. I had a feeling that things wouldn't always be smooth if she lived here.

"Yeah, it would take some getting used to, but she's your

sister. I think it would be good for you to spend some time with her."

I sighed. He was right. "Ok. I'll tell her tomorrow that we'll check with the town to see if it's even a possibility."

We turned off our bedside lamps and lay down. Beside me, Ella was snoring softly. Down the hall, my sister and Mikey were sleeping in their rooms and my parents downstairs. My entire family under one roof. I'd made it through the Christmas season, but I knew the New Year would bring many changes—some good, and some bad. I also knew that together as a family, we could make it through anything.

AUTHOR'S NOTE

Thank you for reading A Killer Christmas Party. I hope you enjoyed spending more time with Jill Andrews and her family. If you did, I'd really appreciate it if you left a review.

For information about my new releases and other exciting news, please visit my website, nicoleellisauthor.com and sign up for my e-mail newsletter.

Sweet Success (Book 2)
Sweet Promises (Book 3)
Sweet Memories (Book 4)
Sweet History (Book 5)
Sweet Matchmaking (Book 6)

Made in the USA
Columbia, SC
11 April 2024

34231954R00102